GOTHAM BALL '54

A Rollickin' Season in the Freaks League

I0552723

JEFF POLMAN

GRASSY GUTTER PRESS • CULVER CITY, CA

ALSO BY JEFF POLMAN

1924 and You Are There!
Ball Nuts
Mystery Ball '58
Twinbill
Red Jacarandas
The Invasion of Normandie
The Porch Roof Classic

Title page photo by Leonard Freed
Author photo by Apple Photo Booth

*This book is dedicated to Michael Dane, one funny fellow
and loyal Freak who left us far too early.*

ISBN: 979-8-218-73674-3

PUBLISHER'S NOTE
This is a work of fiction. Names, characters, places, and incidents drawn
from real life and fantasy baseball have been reimagined by the author
with all good intentions.

BEFOREWORD

The Freaks League, my ongoing adventure in social media using the Strat-O-Matic Baseball board game, features a yearly player draft and general managing from at least a dozen nationwide cohorts. Currently in its 12th season, it includes short game summaries and Photoshopped scoreboard updates at least three times a week.

In some of its campaigns, eccentric "recap reporters" and fictional narratives were generated by the tabletop events. My favorite of these so far was in 2021, with the one that accompanied our 1954 season. The story revolved around three clubs making New York City their home: the Masters of Suspense (Timothy Pike, mgr.) playing in Brooklyn's Rear Window Stadium, the Marilyn DiMaggios (Jack Thompson/Joe Viaene) at the Mr. Coffee Grounds, and Black Lagoons Matter (Scott Bourget/Peter Crapo) in the Bronx, all members of the Ricky & Lucy Division.

Here were the other GMs and their teams:

Ricky & Lucy Division: Bikini Bombs (Jim Surprenant), K2 Summiteers (Tim Lemke), Coonskin Caps (Jim Mikkelsen)

Ozzie & Harriet Division: Brockton Clock Rockers (John Borack), Chrome Run Derbies (Rob Price), Lord of the Big Flies (Donald Gordon), Red Menace (Michael Dane), Flipsides (Darin Orenstein), Blackboard Seven (Keith Shiraki)

All of our seasons are posted in a private Facebook group, but because efforts aren't made on my part to preserve every daily report, I had to painstakingly piece this narrative back together using search windows. For instance, narrator Paulie Dom Rubin's initial brief encounter with Marilyn Monroe, when she stops at his dad's newsstand in search of a *Look Magazine* on either April 23rd or 24th, is missing. Still, the bulk of the story remains, with the first few weeks focused on game action and familiarizing the reader with which players are on which teams, before the multi-character drama kicks into gear around the end of April.

Enjoy the yarn!

—*J.P., Culver City, CA*

PRE-SEASONED

What's crankin', kittens? **Paul Dominic Rubin** here—though you can call me Paulie—and word on the sidewalk is I've been elected to fill in the masses on all the Freaks League doings for this nutty year of 1954. Which oughta be a flat-out cinch, seeing I'll be working Sid's Newsstand at 2nd Ave. and East 84th with my pop Sid Rubin, and we'll have all six New York newspapers all day every day to snatch hardball details and dope from, if you know what I mean.

It's a long, creaky subway ride from our place in Brooklyn but I've been sloggin' it. My mom Paulina, who's Italian and gave me my name and swarthy looks, wants me to get married and get a longshore job on the docks like her dad and uncles had. Mom ain't a big ball fan but Pop makes up for that times five. When Sid was a loyal Yanks rooter back in Ruth and Gehrig and Joe D's days, he went to 1934 Jack Benny Bengough games and later took me to 1948 Hell's Angels games, so he knows Freaks League history better than the inside of his shoes.

Anyway, when I ain't working the stand or having a beer with a pal, I'll try and make a local ball game when I can. Believe me, I've met my share of knock-out dolls at church and synagogue over the years, but there always seems to be one saucy bird dancing her eyes at me from a hot dog stand, know what I mean?

See you on the B-side! —*P.D.R.*

4/5: WHEN ONLY TWO HITS MATTER

Dad and me sat in the upper deck on the first base side at the big Pinstripe Lagoon in the Bronx with 54,438 other people, and saw a tight duel of leftists in Dick Littlefield for the Bikinis and John Antonelli for the BLMs. No one could even generate sawdust until the last of the 5th, when Waitkus bleeded a single, O'Connell and Johnny A. both walked, a Busby grounder clinked off Littlefield's mitt for an error, and a force play by Grady Hatton scored another. Say-Hey Willie Mays then

bombed his first home run to cavernous left field with no one
aboard and the score stayed that way till the end. The Bikini Boys
played with scary fire by putting Bob Milliken and his gopher
ball talents against lefties on the mound for the last two innings,
but somehow all six Lagooners (and their last eleven in a row)
all made outs. "And that's how you steal a ballgame with just two
hits," chirped Dad on our way home.
BKB 000 001 000 - 1 5 1
BLM 000 020 00x - 2 2 0
W-Antonelli-L-Littlefield
HR: Mays

4/6: A FLIPPIN' GOOD ONE

No time for a live ballgame yesterday, because there were
spring sale sections in half of the six New York papers and me
and Dad were busier than autumn squirrels at the newsstand all
day. But that's why having six sports pages to scroll through is
always the dog's bark...

FLIPSIDES 8, BLACKBOARDS 7

The Flophouse mob saw their first win of the year as dramatic
and flippy-floppy as possible. In the top of the 1st, Bob Feller
gave up a Minoso double, Mueller single, Adcock single and
three-run Ray Jablonski dinger [on a 1-2 chance] all in a row, but
a two-run duker by the Duke cut that quick lead in half minutes
later. Feller fired goose eggs his next six innings while the Flips
chipped away at Tom Poholsky. Snider went deep on him his
next time up, added two more singles and drove home five to
become the Star of the Day runner-up, and down 4-3 in the 7th,
the Flops tied the game with three singles, the last one by Nellie
Fox to tie the game at four. Lefty Leo Kiely came on but gave up
a double and two-run single and four runs were home.

The Blackboards weren't chalking up this defeat yet, though.
With Don Mossi on the mound in the 9th, Jablonski singled,
Sammy White walked, and after one out, Ellis Kinder came on

to face pinch-sticker Bob Nieman. He singled off Fox's glove [another 1-2 chance] to make it 7-5. Ron Jackson then pinch-hit, bounced a second sure DP ball to Fox, who booted this one for an error and loaded the bases. Temple got beaned to make it 7-6, Minoso hit a sac fly and we were tied. To the last of the 10th then against Dave Jolly, when Groth and Kennedy both singled with one out, Bridges bounced out and Billy Glynn scorched a single into right-center for the sweaty winner!

BBS 400 000 003 0 - 7 9 1
FLP 200 100 400 1 - 8 12 1
W-Kinder L-Jolly
HRS: Jablonski, Snider-2

RED MENACE 5, CLOCK ROCKERS 0

Okay, so who put fifty clams down in Vegas that Vern Thies would throw the first shutout of the season? Vern walked five Clockers, which is pretty much a cinch against those on-base monsters, but scattered four singles, stranded ten and didn't let the three errors by his fielders bug him one bit. Avila had a pair of RBI singles and Pee Wee smacked a two-run homer and the Milwaukee crowd didn't even feel cold.

CLK 000 000 000 - 0 4 0
RED 001 022 00x - 5 9 3
W-Thies L-Sullivan
HR: Reese
GWRBI-Avila

DERBIES 5, BIG FLIES 4

Make it two straight one-run close shaves for the Chromiums in Cincy. Curt Simmons had the Fly Lords hoodwinked for the first five innings and owned a 4-0 lead on Duane Pillette, but then Gil Hodges woke up. After Irvin and Lopata walked, Doby loaded the bases with a single and Hodges quickly un-loaded them with our first grand salami of the year. But the cool cat Chromes came right back in the 7th with a one-out Delsing triple and deep fly by Gordon to bring in the eventual winner. Irvin tagged Simmons for a leadoff double in the last of the 9th, but Frank Smith and Jim Davis got the final three outs and left him out there.

CRD 200 020 100 - 5 11 0
LBF 000 004 000 - 4 9 1
W-Simmons L-Pillette SV-Davis
HR: Hodges

SUMMITEERS 11, CAPS 5

At the warm Coonskin opener at Final Frontier Field in Boston, the K2s took their ice picks to Virgil Trucks right away. Jackie Robinson hit his first pitch into the left field net, and four runs later, after back-to-back outfield errors by Bruton and Moon, it was 5-0. The Caps did score three on Dean Stone in the 3rd with the help of a Pete Runnels misplay, but Trucks continued to blow his tires, and two singles and four walks in the top of the 5th sent him back to the garage. That crappy Bruton and Moon combo made another pair of two-base errors in the 9th to finish off the humiliation.

K2S 500 030 003 - 11 11 1
CPS 003 001 010 - 5 11 4
W-Stone L-Trucks
HR: Robinson

MASTERS 6, DIMAGGIOS 5

A much closer and far more sluggy opener happened at the Mr. Coffee Grounds in New York. Over half of the hits in the game went for extra bases, and after old Tribe-mates Garcia and Lemon endured volleys of back-and-forth swatting in the middle innings, the game was decided by more bad fielding in the 7th. Red Wilson reached second on a dropped fly by Furillo in right, and when Lemon kicked away an infield single, Wilson raced home with the deciding run.

MOS 001 130 100 - 6 9 0
MDM 001 220 000 - 5 8 3
W-Gracia L-Lemon
HRS: Thomas, Mantle, Rosen

LAGOONS 5, BIKINIS 3

Whitey Ford was slightly better than Billy Pierce, and it made all the difference. Singles by Busby, Musial and Banks and a Bill Sarni sac fly put the Blacks up 2-0 at the start, and a two-run Stan the Man blast in the 3rd jumped it to 4-1. The Bombs made it interesting by bringing home two in the 7th on a Jensen single, Boone triple and scoring grounder by Dropo, but Whitey tightened up, Busby singled home insurance off Howie Fox, and the Pinstripe Lagoon splashed with delight a second straight day.

BKB 001 000 200 - 3 8 1
BLM 202 000 01x - 5 11 2
W-Ford L-Pierce
HR: Musial

4/7: MONTE OPENS DOOR NUMBER THREE

First wins happened for a trio of teams, and only one's still undefeated. My hunch is that the Black Lagoons Matter don't go 162-0, but what do I know?…

BIG FLIES 3, DERBIES 1

Joe Coleman was crusin' along Big Fly Highway with a 3-hit shutout going to the 7th, the only Chrome run off Maglie scoring on a two-base Randy Jackson error in the 4th. Then Lopata drilled a one-out single, Del Ennis pinch-hit a two-out single, and Monte Irvin lofted one high and deep and the heck out of there to left for the only three runs the Flies would need. Hal Newhouser tossed a scoreless 8th and 9th and the Cincy Lord hordes went home happy for the first time.

CRD 000 100 000 - 1 7 0
LBF 000 000 30x - 3 7 1
W-Maglie L-Coleman

SV-Newhouser
HR: Irvin

CAPS 5, SUMMITEERS 4

A back-and-forth war with neither Turley nor Gromek enjoying themselves was 3-2 for the K2s when consecutive boots by Repulski and Robinson, a single and a wild pitch caused two Coonskin runs in the 7th to give them the lead. Then with Narleski on the mound, Burgess doubled with two outs in the 8th, Rivera ran, and jogged home on a single by Hank Thompson for his third hit to tie it at four. Continuing the day's "three theme", the Caps socked three triples, including two right after each other by Amoros and Berra in the 3rd, but it was Bruton's leadoff pinch triple in the 9th that iced the old cake. With Fain at the dish, the next pitch by Turley bounced away from Joe Tipton for a game-winning passed ball!
K2S 110 010 010 - 4 7 2
CPS 002 000 201 - 5 9 1
W-Narleski L-Turley
HRS: Thompson, Mathews

DIMAGGIOS 8, MASTERS 5

I shoulda made it out to the Mr. Coffee Grounds for this one, but the newsstand was hoppin' too much again. The Suspensers mashed three balls out of the park, the Marilyns none, but the DiMaggio hits were bunched up perfectly off Rush, Tremel, and Labine, taking the ballgame with a four-run 5th and a three-run 8th. Bob Porterfield went the distance despite his long ball-itis.
MOS 000 021 011 - 5 9 0
MDM 100 040 03x - 8 9 1
W-Porterfield L-Rush
HRS: Rush, Sauer, Cunningham
GWRBI-Collins
INJURY: Adams-3

CLOCKERS 12, MENACE 6

The Brockton Boys obviously weren't thrilled about getting whitewashed by Vern Thies the game previous, because they made Warren Spahn pray for rain, scoring eight times off him in the first four innings on four singles, three doubles, a beaned Skowron and five walks. Irv Noren had a double and single and knocked in three for the Commies, but the mules were out of the barn, and a dreadful Bob Miller 6th where he gave up a three-run Campanella clout to add to his 5-RBI day meant for more misery in Milwaukee. Batting in the seventh spot, Solly Hemus had two doubles and a triple.

CLK 030 503 100 - 12 14 2
RED 010 210 200 - 6 7 2
W-Pascual L-Spahn
HR: Campanella
GWRBI-Campanella
INJURY: Skowron-5

FLIPSIDES 2, BLACKBOARDS 1

Another tight duel in St. Loo was also the scene of our first injury barrage. The Duke, who bombed two homers the previous game, was plunked on the ankle his first time up by Dickson and put out of action for the day, while Piersall and Atwell also had to leave on the Blackboard side. John Groth took over in center for Snider and drove in Finigan with the first run on a deep sac fly in the 5th. George Zuverink had a shutout going into the 7th, when a Mueller single, Adcock double and plunked Atwell brought on the Flips' relief tag team of Mossi and Kinder. With two gone in the last of the 7th and Harry Byrd pitching, Roy Smalley filling in at second for the injured Temple, booted one. Earl Torgeson pinch-hit a single, Slaughter walked, and when Jolly took the mound, he walked Kiner for the game-clincher. Wild, man!

BBS 000 000 100 - 1 8 4
FLP 000 010 10x - 2 6 0

W-Mossi L-Kiely SV-Kinder
GWRBI-Kiner
INJURIES: Piersall-2, Atwell-3

LAGOONS 4, BIKINIS 1

Black Lagoon pitching completely drowned the Bikini Bomb offense in the three-game sweep in the Bronx, holding them to five total runs and a 1-for-15 performance with runners in scoring position. Jack Harshman was the hurler who treated them harshly this time around, and Dusty Rhodes took care of home business with titanic solo blasts off Early Wynn his first two trips to the plate. Mays hit another one for the Bikinis and drove Musial to the fence with two aboard in the 9th, Stan leaping to snatch the ball and end the game!

BKB 100 000 000 - 1 4 0
BLM 211 000 00x - 4 7 2
W-Harshman L-Wynn
HR: Mays, Hatton, Rhodes-2
GWRBI-Rhodes

4/8: SID'S HOME OPENER IS A GOING-AWAY PARTY

Sure wouldn't wanna be in Sid Gordon's cleats today…

FLIPSIDES 4, DERBIES 2

Down Baltimore way, the Chrome Runners opened the garage doors of Gasoline Alley and delighted the greasy mob for a time with a tight pitching fight between Arnie Portocarrero and Brooks Lawrence. An Andy Carey boot led to to a Flipside run in the 2nd, which held up until Teddy Klu's first bomb of the season sparked a Carey single, Sievers double and Gene Baker pinch sac fly to put the Derbs on top 2-1 in the 6th. Bob Greenwood wasn't as squeaky clean in relief as he was in the season opener, though, and after two shutout innings, he walked Fox to begin the 9th, gave up a Snider single and Joe Frazier creamed a triple for the tying and winning scores! Even more disheartening was the sight of right fielder Sid Gordon limping off the field after badly spraining an ankle running out a grounder to end the 5th. Sid will be lost for a bit over two weeks, which at least will give Wally Post an everyday chance to whack.

FLP 010 000 003 - 4 4 0
CRD 000 002 000 - 2 9 1
W-Kinder L-Greenwood SV-Mossi
HR: Klu
INJURY: Gordon-15

MENACE 4, BIG FLIES 3

Gus Zernial got his first start in the Red Menace cleanup hole against lefty Al Aber and bombed a two-run blast on the first pitch he saw, but after Gus' misplay at first in the 5th, a walk and three singles helped the Flies tie the score at three. No worry. A Yost single, error by Jackson, and Avila single brought in the final digit in the 6th. Erskine chucked well enough for the Menace and Marvelous Marv Grissom added a scoreless 9th against the dangerous top of the Big Fly lineup.

LBF 001 020 000 - 3 8 2
RED 300 001 00x - 4 6 2
W-Erskine L-Aber SV-Grissom
HR: Zernial
GWRBI-Avila

4/9: BIKINI BOMBS AWAY!

On a day of big muscle guys showing off, the Bikinis' home opener at Castle Bravo was sure atomic. Two missed 60% home runs in the last of the 1st happened off Haddix, but one was a Ray Boone triple and the other a Mays sac fly. Then a Smith single and Gilliam double mixed with a two-base-error on Aaron in the 2nd made it 3-0. Then a walk and three singles in the 5th and it was 5-0. Ruben Gomez only had one bad inning, but Coonskin chuckers had two more of the gopher ball kind. Mays, reliever Jackie Collum, and Boone all went deep in the 8th and the rout was history.

CPS 000 000 040 - 4 8 1
BKB 120 020 33x - 11 12 1
W-Gomez L-Haddix
HRS: Mays, Collum, Boone
GWRBI-Mays
INJURY: Aaron-2

SUMMITEERS 8, DIMAGGIOS 7

What looked like another rout when it was 8-3 K2s after six didn't end up that way. McDermott sputtered late and Johnny Sain had to save his squirrelly butt by getting Goodman to ground out with two aboard in the 9th. Hank Thompson was blotto for the K2s with two singles, a double, and homer in his four trips, and DiMag starter Bob Grim only lasted three horrifically grim innings (6 runs and 8 hits)

MDM 102 000 202 - 7 11 1
K2S 114 002 00x - 8 14 1
W-McDermott L-Grim SV-Sain
HRS: Thompson, Vernon
GWRBI-Abrams

MASTERS 5, LAGOONS 2

As you might have seen on last night's dicecast, the Rear Window Stadium home opener in Brooklyn actually did go off without a Hitch, mainly due to Bob Keegan tumbling into the courtyard with a Grim-like performance. His chief nemesis was Hank Sauer, who walloped a two-run upper balcony shot in the 1st and added three more singles for the day. Red Wilson also doubled twice and Don Liddle didn't give the Lagooners a hit until Kaline's RBI triple in the 5th. Back-to-back three-baggers by Banks and Sarni in the 7th brought on the Suspenseful pen, Jim McDonald providing some by walking three straight guys with two outs in the 9th, before pinch-hitter Harmon finally flied out. So I guess no team's having a perfect record again!

BLM 000 010 100 - 2 5 0
MOS 221 000 00x - 5 13 0
W-Liddle L-Keegan SV. McDonald
HR: Sauer
GWRBI-Sauer

BIG FLIES 13, MENACE 2

Hank Bauer topped Mays, Thompson, and Sauer in the Star of the Day slugging race with three singles, a double, and homer in six times to the plate as the Fly Lords racked up 22 hits off Podres, Thies, and Friend and sent the Menace fans off to their daily protests on the early side. Russ Meyer cashed in big time on the swattage, which unbelievably, happened on maybe the coldest day possible in Milwaukee.

LBF 313 310 200 - 13 22 0
RED 000 000 101 - 2 7 1
W-Meyer L-Podres
HRS: Bauer, Seminick
GWRBI-Bauer

DERBIES 4, FLIPSIDES 3

The Chromers edged across the finish line in the 10th for their first win in Gasoline Alley. Wilson and Surkont hadn't had their Wheaties, Joe Frazier following up his winning hit in the last game with a triple and double here, and Carey and Sievers homering back-to-back, but after the Flips tied things with a pinch sac fly by Billy Glynn in the 7th, reliever Jim Davis threw three and two-third scoreless innings to set up the climax against Mossi. Billy Hunter started it with a pinch single with one out, and after Kuenn and Klu both walked, Kinder came in to face Wally Post, filling in for Sid Gordon, who singled up the middle to win it!

FLP 011 000 100 0 - 3 7 0
CRD 100 200 000 1 - 4 9 1

W-Davis L-Mossi
HRS: Carey, Sievers
GWRBI-Post
INJURY: Slaughter-2

CLOCKERS 7, BLACKBOARDS 6

As seen last night by us "dicecast" night owls, the Clock Rockers pulled out another thriller in ten innings on a Solly Hemus double off Kiely. It was a weird one, the Clocks scoring five times in the 1st on Chakales before Bob settled down for his next five innings. The Seven scored six times to take the lead in the 5th after a Minnie Minoso blast tied it, but a second RBI single by Johnny Logan re-tied it in the 7th. Windy McCall was actually the star of the game with four and a third scoreless innings to shut down the Blackboard bats when that kind of thing was needed.

CLK 500 000 100 1 - 7 9 1
BBS 000 420 000 0 - 6 10 1
W-McCall L-Kiely SV-Wilhelm
HR: Minoso
GWRBI-Hemus

4/10: THE FULL MONTE, CHAPTER TWO

So I guess one dramaticky game-winning homer wasn't enough for Mr. Monte Irvin, who waited for the 14th inning to roll around out at Marx Park in Cincy before he bombed another one off Harry Dorish as his Big Flies edged the Menace. It was a weird one altogether, because Art Fowler had a 5-0 lead and two-hit shutout going into the 8th, when Lopata singled, Dittmer got plunked and sent to the infirmary for almost a week, and Lou Limmer pinch-hit a single to fill the bases. That Irvin character singled off reliever Grissom to finally put the Flies on the board, and after a DP grounder brought in another, Doby singled, Hodges belted one over the wall and the score was tied at five!

Then it was a long scoreless duel between Hal Newhouser and Grissom even though both teams blew great chances. In the top of the 12th the Flies had first and third and one out and couldn't score, and in the last of the 13th, the Menace had second and third and nobody out and Yost, Avila and Zernial could not do a dang thing. Reese had two doubles and a single for the Pinkos but it was all for naughts.

LBF 000 000 050 000 01 - 6 10 1
RED 020 100 200 000 00 - 5 15 0
W-Newhouser L-Dorish SV-Brown
HRS: Hodges, Irvin
GWRBI-Irvin
INJURY: Dittmer-6

SEVEN 5, CLOCKERS 4

The Blackboarders evened their series with the Rockers in similar comeback style, though it didn't take nearly as long. A 4-0 lead for Vic Raschi against Garver evaporated by the 4th when Joe Adcock's leadoff blast sparked a three-run rally and two singles and a Jablonski deep fly tied it up the next inning. In the 6th, with two on and two outs, Minoso beat out an infield single that Hatfield also threw wide, scoring the go-ahead and eventual winner. By the way, 46% of the games played so far have been by one run.

CLK 103 000 000 - 4 8 2
BBS 000 311 00x - 5 12 3
W-Garver L-Raschi SV-Jolly
HR: Adcock
GWRBI-Minoso

SUMMITEERS 11, DIMAGGIOS 0

Uhh, this one wasn't. With Willard Nixon spinning a shutout as unlikely as the one Vern Thies did, the K2s triggered an avalanche of hits and runs against Pollet, Purkey, Kuzava, and I guess Marilyn herself. Robinson and Rivera had three hits apiece atop their lineup, and even Nixon singled and doubled in the

onslaught. All but three mountaineers had RBIs in the game.
MDM 000 000 000 - 0 6 2
K2S 020 113 40x - 11 14 0
W-Nixon L-Pollet
GWRBI-Nixon

DERBIES 8, FLIPSIDES 4

Who can put the brakes on Andy Carey? After his single and double off Consuegra to knock in the first four runs of this one, Andy is 12-for-24 on the season with seven RBIs as the Chromiums revved up their offense for a six-run 3rd that also included a three-run moon shot by the not-lollygagging Sherm Lollar. Robin Roberts was his usual efficient self, allowing just two hits and no walks to the Flips before Snider and Frazier went back-to-back in the 7th to make the score semi-interesting.
FLP 000 000 220 - 4 6 0
CRD 206 000 00x - 8 14 1
W-Roberts L-Conseugra
HRS: Snider, Frazier, Lollar
GWRBI-Carey

4/12: BIKINIS GET WHITEY-WASHED

The Bikini Bombs managed to score eleven runs in their fourth game of the year, but have been luckless and blotto the rest of the time, especially against the ruthless southpaws from the Lagoon. This time it was Whitey Ford's turn again, and despite walking four the only hit he allowed was an Al Smith single leading off the Bikini 7th. Early Wynn was putting far more people on base, and he escaped every jam until Dusty Rhodes cleaned his clock for a two-run shot [on a 25% chance] in the 7th. A visit to their local South Pacific voodoo chief might be on the agenda for these "Bombs" soon enough!
BLM 000 000 200 - 2 7 1
BKB 000 000 000 - 0 1 1
W-Ford L-Wynn

HR: Rhodes
GWRBI-Rhodes

CLOCKERS 3, FLIPSIDES 2

Tight, low-scoring duels were also the rage in the Ozzie and Harriet Division, along with wild pitchers, man. Both Zuverink and Sullivan walked a half dozen guys, but the three straight that Zuvie coughed up in the Clocker 6th gave them the two runs that decided the game. Ashburn's two-base error in the 2nd gave the Flips a pair of unearned scores in the 2nd, but the on-base magic of the Brockton Boys was evident again, and they've now taken five of their first seven.
FLP 020 000 000 - 2 6 1
CLK 100 002 00x - 3 5 1
W-Sullivan L-Zuverink SV-Wilhelm
GWRBI-Logan

DERBIES 2, FLIES 1

More simple baseball math here. A Hodges solo smash off Coleman put the Flies up in the 6th, but after hurling a one-hitter of his own through seven, Duane Pillette walked Klu to start the 8th, allowed singles to Sievers and Post, and a deep fly to Lollar to tie the game. After Frank Smith relieved in the top of the 10th with the bases loaded and no one out, Lopata, Bolling, and pinch-hitter Fitz gerald were unable to get the go-ahead run across, setting things up for the Derbs against Hal Brown. With one out, Kuenn singled, Delsing hit a second double and That Man Carey singled in the winner!
LBF 000 001 000 00 - 1 6 0
CRD 000 000 010 01 - 2 7 3
W-Smith L-Brown
HR: Hodges
GWRBI-Carey

MENACE 5, SEVEN 3

A 3-1 lead for Don Johnson and the Blackboards went in

the classroom trash can in the top of the 8th, when Avila led with a single off reliever Harry Byrd for his third hit of the day. Lefty Bob Miller then entered (righty Bob Miller started for the Reds), Gus Zernial hit instead and ripped a single. Jolly replaced Miller but wasn't too happy, as Marsh walked, Tuttle singled, Pafko walked, and with two gone Reese walked and Yost singled and four Menacing runs were across. Grissom threw two scoreless in relief and the the Seven had last place in the division to themselves, which can happen when you allow eight free passes in a game.

RED 100 000 040 - 5 8 1
BBS 000 300 000 - 3 12 0
W-Dorish L-Jolly SV-Grissom
HR: Avila
GWRBI-Reese

4/17: COMMIE INSURRECTION AT THE ROCK SHOP

Well on their way to a 9-3 record out of the gate, Frank Sullivan and the Clock Rockers took a 4-1 lead and four-hitter into the 9th in Detroit, when the Reds suddenly become menacing. Avila and Ward begin with singles to bring on spotless (so far) bullpen ace Hoyt Wilhelm. Noren fouls out, but Tuttle and Pafko single in runs to cut it to 4-3. Seminick is out on a force, but then with their heads on the block, Gus Zernial pinch-hits a clutch single to score Tuttle with the equalizer, Reese follows seconds later with a clutch single of his own, and the Menace have the lead! Grissom then retires Hemus, Williams, and Skowron and the shocking incident is complete.

RED 000 010 004 - 5 10 1
CLK 100 002 100 - 4 6 0
W-Fowler L-Wilhelm SV-Grissom
GWRBI-Reese

FLIPSIDES 9, FLIES 7

In a second straight slugfest seen on last night's dicecast, a homer-filled first three innings pushes the Flips out to a 6-3 lead for Bob Feller, only to have the Flies score four times in the 6th, capped by a Randy Jackson bomb, to take a 7-6 advantage. Undaunted, the Flips flip the game script again, scoring single runs in the 7th, 8th, and 9th off the Lords' bullpen to even the series at a game apiece. Early on, the Duke of Flatbush whacks his fourth and fifth homers and drives in five.

FLP 213 000 111 - 9 12 0
LBF 111 004 000 - 7 12 4
W-Dixon L-Burtschy SV-Mossi
HRS: Snider-2, Dark, Doby, Lepcio, Jackson
GWRBI-Glynn (pinch-hit single)

DERBIES 2, SEVEN 0

Joe Coleman and reliever Bob Greenwood are spot on, and the Chromers eek out another in a series of tight wins to move to a half game behind the Clockers. A Wally Post homer in the 5th and Carey RBI single in the 8th off Don Johnson is all they need.

BBS 000 000 000 - 0 7 1
CRD 000 010 01x - 2 9 0
W-Coleman L-Johnson SV-Greenwood
HR: Post
GWRBI-Post

DiMAGGIOS 3, LAGOONS 1

Whitey Ford pitches well enough to win for the third time, but hittable Joe Nuxhall is far better, holding the Lagooners scoreless until Ruin the Man's Shutout Time in the 9th, forcing Jim Hughes into the game to get Sam Dente on a double play ball with two aboard to end the game. Granny Hamner continues to excel for the Marilyns, singling home their first run and hitting a sac fly later.

BLM 000 000 001 - 1 7 1
MDM 001 010 01x - 3 4 0
W-Nuxhall L-Fors SV-Hughes

HR: Rosen
GWRBI-Hamner
INJURY: O'Connell-5

BOMBS 6, SUMMITEERS 4

Trailing 4-0 to Willard Nixon thanks to a pair of two-run dingers off Wynn, the Bikinis do the Watusi late in the party, scoring six times off Nixon and Johnny "In" Sain for a second consecutive win at Windy Gap Park. Down 4-3 in the 8th, a two-out pinch double by Bill Wilson and three-run Al Smith homer (on a 25% chance) puts them up for good.
BKB 000 001 230 - 6 12 0
K2S 002 020 000 - 4 8 0
W-Loes L-Sain SV-Ridzik
HRS: Smith, Robinson, Vernon
GWRBI-Smith

MASTERS 5, CAPS 3

No late dramatics here, just a crummy Harvey Haddix outing and a two-run Frank Thomas net job in Boston to get the Suspensers going. The Caps tire Don Liddle out in the 6th, but Clem Labine and Jim McDonald keep the rest of their offense at bay.
MOS 210 101 000 - 5 11 1
CPS 000 011 010 - 3 7 2
W-Liddle L-Haddix SV-McDonald
HRS; Thomas, Fain
GWRBI-Thomas

4/20: SUMMITEERS STUCK IN A CREVASSE

Outhitting your opponent 15-6 is a sure way to snap a six-game losing skid, right? Well yeah, unless you lose. Turley takes a 2-0 lead on Grim in a battle of the Bobs at the Mr. Coffee Grounds, before Al Rosen ties it up with a two-run job in the 3rd. A Thompson sac fly puts the Mountaineers back up 3-2 in the 6th, and then Turley comes home to roost—or gets roasted. Two singles, three walks, and two horribly timed errors by Grammas brings in four DiMaggio runs, and the Marilyns merrily bounce their way to another win to put them over .500.

K2S 101 001 002 - 5 15 2
MDM 002 004 02x - 8 6 0
W-Grim L-Turley
HRS: Rosen, Furillo

CAPS 5, LAGOONS 3

And make it five straight drownings for the Lagooners, as Trucks easily out-throws Keegan, the Caps bashing three homers to put them back to within a mere game of first.

CPS 200 201 000 - 5 10 1
BLM 000 030 000 - 3 6 1
W-Trucks L-Keegan
HRS: Berra, Jones, Moon
GWRBI-Berra

BIKINIS 8, MASTERS 6

The Bombs rediscover their lethal weapons and even their first series with the Suspensers at a game apiece. Phil Cavaretta singles twice, homers and knocks in three, and Say-Hey adds a single, double, and triple as Mike Garcia is surprisingly awful.

BKB 013 012 010 - 8 14 0
MOS 000 211 011 - 6 10 0
W-Pierce L-Garcia SV-Loes
HRS: Cavaretta, Hofman
GWRBI-Miranda

SEVEN 6, BIG FLIES 3

The Blackboards scrape their fingernails to within a game of .500 by knocking around Sal Maglie, Jolly notching another save, this time for Garver. Monte Irvin drives in all three Big Fly scores. The Flies get Jack Dittmer back in the lineup and promptly lose catcher Lopata for two weeks.

BBS 201 001 002 - 6 10 0
LBF 000 010 101 - 3 10 1
W-Garver L-Maglie SV-Jolly
HR: White
INJURY:Lopata-15

CLOCKERS 6, DERBIES 5

The Brocktonites become the first team to win ten times as Wilhelm blows a late 5-2 lead and a double, single, and pinch sac fly by Westlake walk it off the stage anyway in the 10th.

CRD 001 100 021 0 - 5 9 0
CLK 211 010 000 1 - 6 13 2
W-Wilhelm L-Lint
HRS: Skowron, Hatfield
GWRBI-Westlake

MENACE 5, FLIPSIDES 1

All Menacing, all day. Podres quiets the Flips on six hits, Avila knocks in three and Yost two with a ding-dong and the Reds take care of business after Pee Wee Reese goes out for a spell.

RED 100 020 020 - 5 10 0
FLP 001 000 000 - 1 6 1
W-Podres L-Byrd
HR: Yost
GWRBI-Avila
INJURY: Reese-3

4/22: ON-BASE GREMLINS RUIN DERBY DAY

Only one ruckus was played yesterday out in Detroit, and it was another rip-snorter...

CLOCKERS 6, DERBIES 5

After Joe Coleman whacks a solo homer off Frank Sullivan to help his own cause in the 3rd, the Rockers apparently take it personally and come back with three in the 4th on three singles and three walks. It stays that way until the 7th, when Klu walks, Siev-

ers singles, and Wally Post crushes one out of the yard. A Delsing triple and Klu sac fly the next inning and it's 5-3 Chromers.

Perfect time for the on-base factory known as the Clock
Rockers to punch in to work. With two outs and no one aboard
against Frank Smith, Johnny Logan squibs a single into center.
Dee Fondy pinch-hits so lefty Jim Davis enters. Fondy walks.
So does Ashburn. So does Hemus. Williams reaches on Kuenn's
second boot of the game to tie the score, and Skowron dunks
in a single for the winner. As if the come-from-ahead loss isn't
enough, despite Sid Gordon coming back in a few days the
Derbs now lose Andy Carey for a solid week. Logan meanwhile
earns Star of the Day for his two-out, nobody aboard squibbler
because he knew…he knew…

CRD 001 000 310 - 5 4 2
CLK 000 300 03x - 6 9 0
W-Sullivan L-Davis SV-Wilhelm
HRS: Coleman, Post
GWRBI-Skowron
INJURIES: Carey-7, Courtney-3

4/25: ANOTHER FLIPPIN' GOOD GAME

No New York teams were playing in town, and the day just
felt different. I was real tempted to call my best pal Bobby Z. to
give him every detail about meeting Marilyn, but then thought
otherwise. Same deal at home. Dad just asked how the day went
and how many papers did we sell, while Mom baked up some
veal cacciatore and bowtie pasta and asked me for the thirteenth
time why I didn't want to call Bianca Ballorino and ask her out.
Sorry Ma, I told her, I don't like blind dates. ("She is not blind,
Paulie!")

At the stand, those new issues of *Look Magazine* showed up,
the one with Mr. and Mrs. Hemingway on the cover, and I made
sure they were right in front of the register just in case. A couple
of store ladies and a rugged guy who was probably a Hemingway fan bought copies, along with this young guy in sunglasses,

a checked sport jacket and felt hat, who grabbed a copy, walked around the block with it, then I guess changed his mind and brought it back. I refunded his fifteen cents, watched him walk off again, then had a sudden thought. Leafed through the copy he returned and a folded up piece of paper fell out:

M.M.—
Hotel Picadilly lobby
SAT- NOON

Gee-zus. I hid the copy with the note inside it under the counter so no one else would buy it. Made sure my hair was combed way back the way girls like it and waited for my special customer to possibly re-appear…

4/26:
SUSPENSERS HARDLY MASTERLY IN MILWAUKEE

Pop left the newsstand to go have lunch down at Mort's Deli. He asked me if I wanted a corned beef to go but I was too nervous to even think about eating.

Ten seconds after he left, Marilyn appeared. She was dressed in a brown skirt, dark glasses, and yellow head scarf, and smelled like cigarettes and cinnamon. I took an extra long time putting the *Look Magazine* I had been hiding into a bag for her.

"So can you tell me who the guy was?"

—"Excuse me?"

"The cool-looking character in the hat who stuck the note in here."

—"I don't think that's your business, sonny."

"It's Paulie. Paulie Dom Rubin. Hi. And this being our family business I kinda like to know our regular customers the best I can. Even you…Miss Monroe."

—"Can I please have my magazine now?"

"Sure. Free of charge. And…I guess Joe won't be wanting his

own copy?"

—"Joe is away in Pittsburgh to watch our team play the Seven Blackboards. I don't think he'll need one."

"Figured as much. Don't worry, okay? I'll keep whatever this was zipped up."

—"You're an angel."

I blushed. "Yeah. I sort of am. And anyway, that team you mentioned is called the Blackboard Seven."

—"Oh. Of course... Thank you!"

She took the magazine bag and hurried off again.

MENACE 9, MASTERS 0

I guess Hitch must be going psycho after seeing the results of this one. Okay, Frank Thomas might be out a few games, but with Mike Garcia facing Carl Erskine, his boys still have more than a fighter's chance at Marx Field to quell the Commies. Except "Oisk" has other ideas, firing a dominating 4-hit shutout while Garcia loses his breakfast and lunch against the Menacing bats and is pummeled out of the game before the third inning ends. Two singles and a walk start the last of the 2nd before Whitey Lockman steps up. Given a try at first base and inserted in the 8-hole, Whitey promptly belts a grand slam. Five singles and four runs later in the 3rd, Garcia is dispatched to the wet room and the Reds coast from there. Somehow, Garcia, by all accounts one of the best pitchers in the league, is now saddled with a 1.541 WHIP and 7.11 E.R.A. in his 27 innings.

MOS 000 000 000 - 0 4 1
RED 044 100 00x - 9 13 0
W-Erskine L-Garcia
HR: Lockman
GWRBI-Lockman

SEVEN 9, DiMAGGIOS 2

Nearly the same fate happens to the slumping DiMaggios (Sorry, Marilyn!), who nearly get whitewashed by Tom Poholsky if not for a Rosen double and Collins dinger during Ruin the Guy's Shutout in the Ninth Time. Minoso and Jablonski go batty for the Blackboards, Minnie with two singles, a double, triple, and four knocked in, and Ray with three singles and two walks in his five at bats. For the road team, Bob Grim has been even worse than Garcia, now 1-3 with a 2.296 WHIP and 9.18 E.R.A. Yowch!

MDM 000 000 002 - 2 7 0
BBS 200 303 10x - 9 17 0
W-Poholsky L-Grim
HR: Collins
GWRBI-Minoso

BIKINIS 5, CLOCKERS 1

Less of a wipeout but no less impressive are the Bombs taking care of Vic Raschi in their home dicecast debut. Early Wynn throws a fine six-hitter and climbs out of many jam jars despite six walks. Mays clubs his eighth homer to put the Bikinis ahead for good in the 3rd and it comes moments after he nails Ashburn at the plate to end the top of the inning. With the win, the Bombs reach .500 for the first time and like everyone in both divisions, is officially in the race.

CLK 001 000 000 - 1 6 1
BKB 002 000 12x - 5 10 0
W-Wynn L-Raschi
HR: Mays
GWRBI-Mays

DERBIES 2, SUMMITEERS 1

The Chromers finally take another game and shock of all shocks, it's a tight, low-scoring one. Curt Simmons gives up a single, homer and double to Bob Cerv, a single to Robinson and absolutely nada to anyone else, as a Kell double and Klu single off Dean Stone in the 6th bring home the eventual winner. Without Mathews in powerless Baltimore, the K2s are pretty handicapped.

K2S 000 100 000 - 1 4 0
CRD 100 001 00x - 2 7 0
W-Simmons L-Stone
HR: Cerv
GWRBI-Klu

LAGOONS 9, BIG FLIES 6

It's another Dusty Rhodes Day, as the big guy doubles in the 1st off Pillette, walks during a three-run rally in the 4th to give the Lagoons the lead, then wallops a grand slam off Hal Brown in the 5th to all but put the game away. Jack Harshman is treated harshly early on, but recovers big time and sets down 14 Big Flies in a row at one point before Jim Hearn finishes up and gets his final eight guys.
LBF 030 000 300 - 6 6 1
BLM 110 340 00x - 9 10 0
W-Harshman L-Pillette SV-Hearn
HR: Rhodes
GWRBI-Hatton

CAPS 8, FLIPSIDES 6

The Flips battle back throughout against Minner, but the extra-base attack by the Coonskins is just too much for them. Portocarrero serves up five doubles, a triple and two homers in his five and two-thirds of lousy work, and Ferris Fain triples late for their ninth extra-base job. Henry Aaron, a dashing but skinny young rookie for the Caps, doubles twice and singles in his first three at bats and gets intentionally passed his next time up. The boy has a future!
CPS 101 221 010 - 8 16 0
FLP 110 100 201 - 6 13 1
W-Minner L-Portocarrero SV-Narleski
HRS: Amoros, Fain
GWRBI-Fain

4/27: COMEBACK KIDS ALL OVER THE JOINT

You knew I was gonna do this, right? Saturday came along and I zipped down to Times Square before noon to stake out the lobby at the Picadilly. Kept a Black Lagoons Matter cap low over my eyes and parked myself behind a tall ferny plant with a good view of the room. The cat with the checked sport coat and felt hat appeared a few minutes after me and sat on a couch bouncing his leg and staring at the door.

Marilyn showed up ten minutes late. She had a different-colored scarf over her head and different dark glasses but I knew it was her because Checked Coat Cat hopped up immediately without a word and walked her to the elevators. No one else recognized her which was kind of amazing seeing what a star she is, but she also came in quick through a back door. Anyway, being the snoop that I am, hurried over to the elevator they disappeared into alone and watched the arrow thing rise up until it stopped at the 14th floor. I grabbed the elevator next to it and punched 14.

It wasn't the fanciest hotel, kind of quiet, which I figured was perfect for whatever might be going on. I crept past every closed door, ears tuned up like a bloodhound's. Then I heard a breathy, giggly voice behind 1412 at the end of the hall. It had to be Marilyn's. I moved right up, put my ear to the door—

And a large hand grabbed me by the collar that was attached to a larger voice.

—"What the hell are you doing, punk??"

It was a red-faced guy in a dark suit that was either the house dick or Marilyn's. Before I could get a word out the door was thrown open and she stood there looking at me, the Checked Coat Cat behind her with his sunglasses and coat off, holding what looked like sheets of music in his hand.

—"You!" Marilyn cried.

"I'm sorry!" I sputtered, "I'm just a big fan, and I was worried about you, and thought you might be in trouble!"

—"You're in trouble alright!" said the brute, and he whirled me around by the collar like I was a side of beef.

—"WAIT!" said Marilyn, "It's okay. I know this boy." She dropped her voice at me and smiled. "Everything's fine. It's not what you're probably thinking. I'll come find you later and explain, okay? Promise."

The brute let go and stood there until I walked back toward the elevators. I heard the door close again and all I could stew about was 'Boy?' Are you kidding me??

BIG FLIES 5, LAGOONS 4

Four of the six games yesterday featured late comebacks, and none more dope than the one over in the Bronx which I'm glad my dad missed. Sal Maglie and Bob Keegan are locked in a tight little back-and-forth battle, Hodges smacking two dingers and Rhodes adding another one. Keegan is given a chance to finish after throwing a fine 7th and 8th, but Ted Lepcio doubles off him to start the 9th. In comes Tom Hurd, who retires Fitzgerald and Dittmer, and up steps Del Ennis to pinch-hit. Out goes the baseball into the left field bleachers for a real big fly, and the Lords have the lead! With Newhouser already used, Moe Burtschy comes on for the Flies, gets the first two outs and then Kaline, who had gone in for Rhodes, whacks a double. Musial crushes one deep to right-center that just misses leaving the yard, and Kaline flies around third, but Larry Doby erases him at the plate on a 70% safe chance to end the game!
LBF 101 001 002 - 5 9 1
BLM 012 010 000 - 4 11 0
W-Newhouser L-Hurd SV-Burtschy
HRS: Hodges-2, Ennis, Rhodes
GWRBI-Ennis

DiMAGGIOS 4, SEVEN 2

Well, at least Joe was probably happy today, watching his pitcher Pollet mostly mow down the Blackboards in Pittsburgh.

Howie does allow two unearned scores in the 1st, but hurls a 3-hit shutout from there, while the Marilyns chip away with single runs on Don Johnson in the 4th and 8th to tie it up. Then Dave Jolly does his wild stuff again to ruin the day for the home crowd, loading the bases on walks, giving up a two-run single to Mantle and walking another before he's yanked off the mound with a vaudeville cane. "Not So" Jolly somehow has six saves to lead the league, yet is also 0-5 with a 7.06 E.R.A. and 21 walks in 15 innings. Nails on a blackboard, for sure.

MDM 000 100 012 - 4 9 1
BBS 200 000 000 - 2 5 0
W-Pollet L-Jolly
GWRBI-Mantle

MASTERS 6, MENACE 4

Out in Milwaukee, Johnny Podres is given the lead when the Reds score three times in a rush off Bob Rush in the 3rd, but Johnny can't handle it, and that annoying powerful fellah named Sauer crushes his 11th homer with two aboard in the 5th to put the Suspensers ahead for good. Hoak adds a two-run single the next inning, and the Masters stay on the hot heels of the Caps atop the Ricky & Lucy.

MOS 010 032 000 - 6 9 2
RED 003 000 010 - 4 11 0
W-Rush L-Podres SV-McDonald
HR: Sauer
GWRBI-Sauer

DERBIES 8, SUMMITEERS 6

The starting version of Dave Jolly has to be Bob Turley, who is now 0-4 with 21 walks in 27 innings for the K2s, after the Chromers come back from a 6-4 deficit to bury him with an avalanche of four runs in the 7th, capped by a two-run Wally Post single. Earlier, Hank Thompson belts a 1st inning grand slam off Coleman, but Turley's four walks and a Kuenn double put the Derbs right back in the game an inning later. The K2s might be missing Mathews big time, but their lack of reliable pitching outside of Willard Nixon has really done them in lately.

K2S 400 020 000 - 6 10 2
CRD 030 001 40x - 8 8 0
W-Davis L-Turdley
HRS: Thompson, Vernon
GWRBI-Post

CLOCKERS 4, BIKINIS 3

Johnny Schmitz goes to 4-0 and the Clockers snap a late 1-1 tie at Castle Bravo with three runs in the 8th off Gomez, Collum, and Loes. The Bombs come right back with two of their own, but can't manage the equalizer in the 9th despite two straight powerful pinch-hitters and a radioactive breeze blowing out to left. The narrow win puts the Brocktonites a full game and a half ahead of the FOUR second place .500 teams in the Ozzie & Harriet.

CLK 001 000 030 - 4 7 0
BKB 001 000 020 - 3 9 3
W-Schmitz L-Gomez
GWRBI-Skowron

CAPS 10, FLIPSIDES 2

No drama in this one, just a thorough mauling by the Coonskins, who in the early going lead the league with a .304 team average and 0.860 OPS. Amoros (two-run shot in the 1st) and Aaron (single and homer) stay hot, but no one is more scorchy than Willie Puddinhead Jones, who raises his average to .333 with three singles, a double, and homer off Wilson, Dixon, and mop-up man Al Corwin.

CPS 212 100 202 - 10 18 2
FLP 001 010 000 - 2 7 1
W-Trucks L-Wilson
HRS: Amoros, Jones, Aaron
GWRBI-Amoros

4/28: NATIONAL NEGRO TREASURES

Meeting Marilyn in a dark back booth at Wally's Lunch on 64th Street was my idea. It had to be dark because if even one person with a camera recognized her, there would be press people all over her like ants in minutes. And she disguised herself with the third different scarf I'd seen her in.

—"Thanks for understanding, Paulie. I'm actually supposed to be out in Los Angeles now working on a new picture for Fox—a musical—and Randall who you saw at the hotel is my singing coach. He lives here, you see, but I didn't want Joe to know I was meeting with him because, well, Mr. DiMaggio just hates the movie business."

"That sure is too bad."

—"Golly, I know! He thinks I'm still out in Hollywood while he travels around with our baseball team, and I have people tell him I'm tied up whenever he tries to call. It's awful distressing, actually."

"Any way I can help?"

—"Oh you're so sweet, but not really. It's just good to have a new 'non-movie' friend I can moan about my problems to. Are you a big baseball fan?"

"You bet your bu—I mean your life I am!"

—"Well, maybe I can talk Joe into leaving you some free tickets at the Mr. Coffee Grounds. I went to a game or two, but I got kind of bored."

"That would be a gas if he could do that, thanks. And I'll be sure to see every new movie you make from now on."

She flashed a smile, then suddenly looked around with a worried expression and gathered her things.

—"I need to skedaddle, Paulie. Thanks for the cherry lime rickey." She leaned in and gave me a little red lipstick peck on the cheek before hurrying out a back exit.

I wouldn't be washing my face for a while.

4/29:
SUMMITEERS CAPTURE CLIFFHANGER
AT CLOCK ROCK SHOP

Only a pair of ballgames in Detroit and St. Louis yesterday
and Joe D. was on his way to Milwaukee to see his boys take on
the Menace, so even though I was tempted to blab about my
Marilyn encounter to Mom and Pop and every friend I had, I
kept my trap zipped.

It wasn't easy. Especially when I was standing in a matinee line
with Bobby Z. outside the Walker Theater in Brooklyn, and he
started grilling me about Bianca Ballorino and whether I had
asked her out yet. I said no, I wasn't thinking about girls at the
moment and he looked at me like I had a faucet sticking out of
my cheek.

—"You're not thinking about Bianca? She's a baby doll!"

"I know, but it's probably because my mom is the one trying to
hitch us up."

—"Oh, I get it…In that case, can ya give me her number?"

Bobby Z. Such a girl mooch. I told him I'd think about it.
Then we went in to watch "Demetrius and the Gladiators" with
Victor Mature, and it took my mind off girls altogether.

5/1: IT'S EARLY, BUT A NICE WYNN

I was the toast of our dice game in the alley off Albany Avenue when I got back to town. I'm sure Bobby Z., Vin Pascarelli,
Donny Gold and Luther the shoeshine kid would have gotten
all hot and bothered hearing my Marilyn Monroe story or about
the strange guy who seemed to be watching me on the train who
might have been related, but I wasn't spilling one bean. All they
cared about was the wild game at the Rock Shop with the nine
home runs and in particular, what Jackie Robinson's three were
like. In truth they were all quick line drives but I added some
dramatic touches because hell, the game wasn't on the tube in

New York and none of them read newspapers.

The problem with keeping something like the Marilyn stuff inside, though, is that it tends to tighten up your innards after a while. Seeing creepy guys in dark glasses watching you does too, but thankfully that hasn't happened since I got back to town. Anyway, it's May now, the flowers are coming out in Prospect Park, the air is sweeter, and the local dolls are suddenly looking more dollish. Funny how that happens.

5/2:
PUTTING RUNNERS ABOARD AND
SCORING THEM MATTERS

Pop gave himself a day off and went to the Black Lagoons game in the Bronx yesterday while I was slaving away at the newsstand with Schnozzo, and it wasn't the best time of his life. Matter of fact he couldn't even eat his brisket cacciatore when he got home that night, which is his favorite thing Mom makes.

—"It's just a stupid baseball game, Sid," she began.

"Like hell it is! How many times did I see the Yazernauts mediocre their way to an 81-81 season during the 1961 Freaks League? And how about them 2003 Cold Stone Stunners? Bums finished with 94 losses and now the Black Lagoons are three games under! I'm tellin' ya I can't catch a break in that ballpark when the Yanks aren't using it!"

—"But Pop, I thought the score was just 2-1 today."

"Think that matters? The Chrome Derbies hit worse than us, and we still got one less run. Outside of Stan the Man, we stink like old borscht against lefties, and Curt Simmons turned us into sissies this time. Plus crummy Bob Keegan, who's 0-4 for us now, pitched his gonads off and got no support."

—"Eat your broccoli, Paulie. You weren't at the game."

"Hell, I knew the thing was over in the 1st when Sid Gordon hit a two-run shot on a 1-4 chance and Musial missed a 1-14 homer in the bottom of the inning!"

—"What are you talking about, Pop?"

"Never mind. Thankfully they hit the road now to visit a couple of those big home run parks in Detroit and Cincy, so maybe they'll pour some pepper in their underwear…And pass the salt, Paulina."

5/3: GRACE KELLY'S IN DEMAND, AND NOT JUST BY HOLLYWOOD

Pop always tells me that Memorial Day is when the pennant races start to sort themselves out, but that the beginning of May always makes for a good sneak preview. If that's true, then we got a full-blown creature feature going on right down Flatbush Avenue, and Pop's Black Lagoons aren't even involved…

MASTERS 8, SEVEN 1

Yep, Hank Sauer Power now has 15 home runs in 24 games, and four games in a row with one. And that ain't the half of it. After the Blackboards scratch two singles and two walks off Bob Rush for a top of the 1st run, Murray Dickson retires his first two Masters of the day. Then Red Wilson doubles, then Sauer doubles, then Frank "White Hurt" Thomas puts one in the upper deck and it's 3-1 for the home crowd. Nothing important happens again until the last of the 5th, when Bell leads with a single, Ray Katt (who went in for an injured Wilson), slams a homer. Then Sauer slams #15. Then after Harry Byrd replaces Dickson, Thomas puts another one in orbit for their third straight dinger, and the Suspensers roll the Seven like steak knives through a stick of butter. At eight games above .500 now, I'm starting to believe these boys got legs. We sure know their hitting coach Grace Kelly does.

BBS 100 000 000 - 1 5 0
MOS 300 040 01x - 8 13 1
W-Rush L-Dickson
HRS: Thomas-2, Katt, Sauer (#15)
GWRBI-Thomas

INJURY: Wilson-2

5/6: DON'T INSULT THE WHITE HURT, PLEASE

"Hey bookworm!" yelled Pop, "We got papers to sell!"

I snapped shut the copy of *Glamour* magazine with a cover story on Marilyn I'd been flipping through behind the register. A color photo of DiMaggio with a bunch of his cronies at some New York restaurant had been circulating around, and because I'm one of those paranoid people I was sure they were talking about me. His ball team was back in town and losing a little too much over at the Mr. Coffee Grounds, but *Glamour* did tell me that Marilyn was back in Hollywood getting ready to film "There's No Business Like Show Business" with Ethel Merman, so at least she wasn't stopping by the newsstand again anytime soon. Someone other than me must have seen her meeting with that wimp of a singing coach, though, and I'd bet you a King Kong Keller bubble gum card he would spill the beans that I saw her too if Joe got ahold of him. All I'm saying is that it was getting hard to concentrate every time I had to make change for a five.

5/8: GO WES, YOUNG MAN

On my way to the train after last night's great game at the Mr. Coffee Grounds, I passed a gaggle of fans waiting for autographs outside the little players' parking lot. I heard this kid complaining he didn't know what Wes Westrum looked like, but I wasn't going to be able to help him much so was about to keep walking but then stopped on a dime.

A big shiny Cadillac was waiting next to the exit with the license plate reading CLIPPER-5, and I knew who that was for. I wanted to run but was kind of frozen, and then this big driver climbed out from behind the wheel to stretch. A couple fans yelled "Where's Joe?" and he waved them away. Then he saw me standing there and walked closer.

Hell if it wasn't the same beefy security guy who grabbed me outside Marilyn and that singing coach's door at the Picadilly Hotel!

—"What are you doin' around here, kid?"

"Same as everyone, leaving the game. What are YOU doing here? Thought you were paid to watch Marilyn!"

—"Guy can't have a second gig? One don't know about the other, so don't go blabbin' it. Matter of fact I'd scram before the Clipper comes out and asks me who you are. He's a little suspicious that way."

Believe me, it was the fastest I ever scrammed.

5/9: SAY HEY HEY HEY!

For probably the tenth time, me and Bobby Z. and Vin Pascarelli and Donny Gold and Luther met up at Solly's Donuts yesterday morning to decide once and for all who the best center fielder in baseball was. The votes were two for Mays, two for the Duke, and one for Mantle. Luther was convinced Bill Tuttle would be better than all of them in a year or two, and then Vin had to ruin my day by bringing up Joe DiMaggio as "probably the best ever".

"No way" I said, "I'd take Tris Speaker."

They looked at me like I had horns on my head.

—"You got something against the Clipper, Paulie?"

"Uhh, not at all. My dad used to see Speaker play though, and—"

—"He was on Boston!" cried Bobby.

"Yeah, and also Cleveland, and Philadelphia! What you got against Beantown?"

—"You actually have to ask me that?"

I told them forget it already, and went back to my jelly glazed.

And then something happened out in Detroit to settle the whole argument.*

*Mays hit three home runs there

5/10: SAUER GRAPES EVEN GROW AT HIGH ALTITUDES

With the Masters wreaking more havoc out in Cleveland and the Lagoons swimming around Boston, the Marilyns were the only local team in town last night, so Pop put their radio broadcast on our living room RCA, which didn't make Ma too thrilled when she decided she wanted to watch the Ernie Kovacs Show in that room for the first time ever. Lucky for Pop, Donny Gold had one of those new Regency transistor radios, and I was borrowing it for a few days. So before you knew it, we were sitting out on our fire escape with the game and a couple bottles of Moxie, enjoying the action. Sometimes the modern age is just a gas.

It also happened to be a good battle. Ruben Gomez and the Bikinis had an early 2-0 lead that was soon 3-1, but Joe Collins tied things up with a two-run belt in the 6th.

—"Did they give a Lagoons score yet?"

"Yeah they're up 6-1 after three. Rhodes hit a grand slammer."

—"Thattaway, you Dusty!" he yelled, loud enough to alarm the neighbors.

The Caps had swept the Lagoons in the Bronx when they were in town last, so Pop was thrilled they might be returning the favor in Beantown. Anyway, at the Mr. Coffee Grounds, Hamner singled in Rosen, who led the Marilyns' 8th with a double, and in the 9th, Howie Pollet gave up a single and two walks but Jim Hughes nailed down the save, and Joe D's team won again. Pop didn't care all that much, not being a DiMaggio fan.

—"Good for the Clipper. But he was no Tris Speaker, that's for sure."

"I know, Pop. You told me that."

—"Did they give the Lagoon score again?"

"Probably. But you were too busy talking and I missed it."

—"Don't be such a smart-aleck."

We could make out the dark light towers at Rear Window

Stadium about five blocks away, and it made me suddenly nervous to find out what those Masters were doing…

5/11: TELL THEM WILLIE MAN IS HERE

Luther called me early yesterday morning before I even had a piece of egg in my mouth.

—"Hey Paulie! Meet us at 80 St. Nicholas Place in Harlem at 9 a.m.!"

"Meet who?"

—"Everybody! You're the last brother I hadda call."

"What's going on?"

—"Get there and see!"

Pop got Schnozzo to help him open the stand, so I could jump on a bunch of trains to Harlem to see what the big deal was.

And it was a deal I won't soon forget. Luther and his Harlem friends were playing a game of morning stickball on big wide St. Nicholas like they always do, and who was there to join 'em this time? The Say-Hey Kid, Willie Mays! Yup, in town this weekend to face the DiMaggios, Willie stopped by for some extra long batting practice. Me and Bobby Z. and Donny Gold stood on the sidewalk with our mouths open like idiots, watched Luther's friends fight over who was gonna be on Willie's team, then watched Willie smack at least three balls halfway to West 150th Street.

"Hey Willie!" I yelled after he ran around the upside down pie tins they were using for bases, "How ya like playing for them Bikini Bombs?"

"Ain't bad!" he yelled back in his funny high voice, "If that Sauer son-of-a-gun ever cools off, we might have a chance! Who's your team, kid?

"Uhhh, don't really got one. I just like baseball."

"Don't we all, man. Don't we all."

He put a hole in a car's back window with his next swing, yelled "UH-OH!" and ran off down the street with Luther and the other kids. Sure glad I snapped a photo of him when I did!

5/13:
ALVIN DARKNESS AT THE EDGE OF FLIPSIDES TOWN

I had another day off from the stand, so left Ma a belated bunch of flowers and hopped on a bus to Yonkers Raceway with Bobby Z. for some afternoon horse betting. I wasn't a big gambler but Bobby had a tip on a thoroughbred named Finger Pie and was filling my ear about it for days until I broke down and said I'd bet on him too.

The odds were 7-1 so we each dropped a ten-spot and made 70 bucks, and we were feeling so lucky and braggy after that we walked right into the Dirt Track Club for a celebratory Ballantine. Right as this tall, Italian guy in a brown silk suit and smoking a cig exited past us and brushed my arm.

"Hey watch it, Mac!" I said, right before I realized the guy was Joe DiMaggio himself! He turned, stared at me like I was a bug under his shoe. Bobby Z punched my arm and after blurting out "Oh—sorry!" I also said, "We're rooting for your team, Joe! It's still early!"

He had two big, ugly guys in suits with him, and he dropped his cigarette and crushed it out.

"You got that right, kid," he said, and they kept walking.

Neither Bobby Z. nor me remember drinking our beers.

CLOCKERS 10, FLIPSIDES 9

If the Clockers end up winning the division by one game, they'll remember this one, and if the Flipsides lose the division by one game, they'll remember this one and kill themselves. Winless Vic Raschi takes the hill in a St. Louis park more suited for him and it still doesn't help. After getting a 2-0 lead he gives up one in the 4th and four in the 5th. Johnny Logan then belts a three-run smash off equally bad Jim Wilson in the 6th to tie the game at five. Never fear, Raschi's still here. With two on and two outs in the bottom of the inning, Fox singles, Slaughter crushes a three-run homer and the Flips flip the scoring script to go up 9-5.

Kinder allows doubles to Williams and Skowron to make it 9-6, and after Corky Valentine(!) thankfully spells Vic and throws two 1-2-3 relief innings, Mossi gets pinch stick Westlake out to start the 9th. Ashburn triples but Michaels whiffs and Mossi is just one out away. But an easy ground ball to Dark bounces off his unshaven face for an error and a 9-7 game. Skowron walks and up steps pinch-hitter Jim Fridley, who won the now-famous slugfest in Detroit against the K2s a few weeks back with an extra inning single. Fridley puts the first pitch in the left field bleachers [on a 1-6 chance], Wilhelm throws a 1-2-3 9th, and the worst loss of the year for practically any team in the league is in the books. [For what it isn't worth, the Flips also miss three 1-15 hit rolls during the game and become the first team to lose 20 times.]

CLK 200 003 014 - 10 11 1
FLP 000 144 000 - 9 11 1
W-Valentine L-Mossi SV-Wilhelm
HRS: Logan, Fridley, Slaughter
GWRBI-Fridley
INJURY: Hatfield-7

MASTERS 13, LAGOONS 2

At least the hideousness of this game is gotten out of the way early. Following up their 14-run, 17-hit attack against the K2s in Cleveland, the Monsters of Suspense® rack up 13 runs and 18 more hits in the Bronx to ruin a great Garcia vs. Ford matchup and send Whitey packing after just three innings. Right now the Suspensers could barf into their hands and turn it into run-scoring hits. Their 26 base runners for the game include eight walks, while the Lagoons don't walk once against Garcia and put only eight aboard, both of their runs on a single and homer by Rhodes. Sauer has been out of this world, but the Masters are also getting huge support from nearly everyone on the roster, such as Frank Thomas (.311), Gus Bell (.325), Red Wilson (.347) and Ray Katt (.371). They have to cool down at some point, don't they?

MOS 033 202 300 - 13 18 0
BLM 000 001 010 - 2 8 0
W-Garcia L-Ford
HRS: Hofman, Katt, McDougald, Rhodes
GWRBI-Hofman

5/14: BEATDOWNS ARE TOUGH TO DIGEST

Two mornings in a row Pop couldn't eat his bacon and cheddar omelette. He sat slumped in his chair like a survivor from Anzio.

—"We threw Ford and Antonelli at them and we weren't in either game."

Of course, he was talking about the Black Lagoons' second straight butchering yesterday at the hands and claws of the Suspense Masters, or Monsters, or Barbarians, or whatever you feel like calling 'em.

—"We're 0-5 against them! How are we even going to compete?"

"Whaddya want me to say, Pop? They're good."

He pounded the table with his fork, rattling Ma's coffee cup.

—"Good?? They're not just good. They're from another planet. On a last-minute hunch they start this *meshuggeneh* at first base named Don Bollweg, and all he does is take Antonelli out of the yard for a 3-0 lead before I even get the relish on my dog!"

"Whaddya want me to say, Pop?"

—"Meantime we can't hit Bob Stinkin' Rush with a boat paddle, and if a 5-0 lead isn't enough for them, they score seven more times off three of our so-called relievers in the 8th! I would've left on the train early but I was too stunned to move a butt cheek."

"Whaddya want me to say, Pop?"

—"Thank God for Ruin the Man's Shutout in the 9th Time

when we scored three, even though there were maybe 55 fans left and a dozen meatheads from Brooklyn making noise in the bleachers. And we got two left in this lousy series. It's a horror movie!"

"Whaddya want me to say, Pop?"

5/15: DRASTIC MEASURES IN THE RICKY & LUCY

When I got back to the newsstand after lunch, Schnozzo yanked me behind the register.

—"Dunno what's wrong with your dad, but somethin' is. He listened to one inning of the Masters and Lagoons game on the radio, said he hadda go visit Madame LeTorque in Times Square and plain took off!"

I knew about Madame LeTorque, or at least walked by her weird-looking shop on 44th Street enough times.

"What the heck happened in the first inning?"

—"You don't wanna know."

I told Schnozzo I'd be back as soon as I could and hopped on a passing bus down to the Square.

MADAME LeTORQUE, FORTUNE TELLER AND SORCERY HISTORIAN read the words on the glass window. I burst in the door. The Madame, in her multi-colored head scarf, too many necklaces, rings and bracelets and too much makeup, was sitting across from a nervous middle-aged woman, reading her palm.

"Was my pop in here??"

—"Excuse me young man!"

"An older guy who looks like me, maybe babbling about a baseball game?"

She hesitated, so I knew he'd been there.

—"Madame LeTorque does not reveal her secrets or client wishes. You have to leave."

"Okay, but did he say anything about the first inning of the Black Lagoons game?"

She rolled her big mascara eyes.
—"You don't want to know."

MASTERS 7, LAGOONS 2

The Monsters only score seven runs this time, but reach back into their magic sack of voodoo and mojo to make them happen. Stupidly assuming the big left field distance at the Pinstripe Lagoon will hurt their righty-powered lineup, three of those righties club four home runs anyway [two on 1-4 rolls and two on 1-6 rolls], and Don and his Liddle friends easily dispatch Eddie Lo-splat and the BLMs for a third straight day (outscoring them 34-7) to go 6-0 against them on the season. Since splitting a twinbill with the Red Menace back on April 28th, the Masters have gone 15-2. The only inkling of mortality in this one comes when shortstop Bobby Morgan gets hurt for five games. Naturally, Jim Brideweser [and his 4e48 defense rating) takes his place, makes the final play of the game and triples in his only at bat. I think Pop is on to something.
MOS 411 000 100 - 7 9 0
BLM 001 001 000 - 2 6 0
W-Liddle L-Lopat
HRS: McDougald-2, Renna, Morgan, Waitkus
GWRBI-McDougald
INJURY: Morgan-5

BOMBS 7, SUMMITEERS 6

That Mays Man drives in three more, with a sac fly, single, double, and triple, and after Rip Repulski ties the score off Gomez with a three-run shot in the 8th, Willie's two-bagger after a leadoff walk to Jensen by Sain in the 9th gives him his tenth game-winner, two more than Sauer Power has.
K2S 300 000 030 - 6 7 0
BKB 100 002 301 - 7 12 2
W-Ridzik L-Sain
HR: Repulski
GWRBI-Mays

DiMAGGIOS 2, CAPS 0

Pretty effective brew at the Mr. Coffee Grounds: Bob Grim isn't terrible, and Hamner and Mantle start the bottom of the 1st with a double and homer for all the scoring off Minner in the game. The win also nudges the Marilyns into a fifth-place tie with the sliding K2s.

CPS 000 000 000 - 0 8 1
MDM 200 000 00x - 2 6 1
W-Grim L-Minner SV-Hughes
HR: Mantle
GWRBI-Mantle
INJURY: Crandall-2

SEVEN 5, DERBIES 4

After two days spent in losing detention, the Blackboards play see-saw in the Forbes Yard with the Chromers to snap their four-game win streak, and beat them by…wait for it…one run! A Temple single ignites a game-tying rally in the 6th against Lawrence, before Johnny singles again in the 7th and scores on a Mueller double. But the recently relentless Derbs take the lead back on a two-run Carey single off Garver in the 8th. No problem. Against Frank Smith and Jim Davis, a walk and two singles in the last of the 8th are followed by Temple's third straight hit, a go-ahead double! Two outs in the top of the 9th, more Chrome shine happens when Bobby Young pinch-hits a single, Kuenn singles, brand new Blackboard third-sacker Hank Thompson boots one in his first start to load the bases, and Gordon walks in a run. Bob Miller comes on to face Ted Klu, who somehow flies to center with the bases stuffed to end it.

CRD 100 000 021 - 4 10 0
BBS 000 001 13x - 5 10 2
W-Garver L-Smith SV-Miller
HR: Gordon
GWRBI-Temple

BIG FLIES 6, MENACE 5

Not as sickening as the Flipsides' last-minute flop to the Clockers the other day, but pretty dang bad. Podres is given a seemingly cozy 5-2 lead on Maglie, but the Flies fight back on a Doby solo shot in the 7th, a two-out Fitz gerald single in the 8th off Grissom, and in the 9th against Spahn, a single, two walks, and a two-out, TWO-run Fitz gerald single that trots it off for a sweep of the series! Stan Lopata gets hurt for the third time this year, but the way Fitzie has been hitting, it's a godsend. For the game, the Menace leave 17 runners on base, while Yost and Avila each miss a 75% ballpark home run chance.

RED 021 011 000 - 5 15 2
LBF 000 200 112 - 6 10 1
W-Bishop L-Spahn
HR: Doby
GWRBI-Fitz gerald
INJURY: Lopata-5

FLIPSIDES 4, CLOCKERS 2
CLOCKERS 16, FLIPSIDES 4

After Feller and Kinder survive some late Clocker uprisings to take their first game against them following five losses, the Flips have a 4-0 lead in the nightcap against Brewer when Sonny Dixon breaks like a cheap blues guitar. A three-run Teddy Ballgame homer ties it in the 5th, and after three one-out singles knock him from the mound in the 7th, Skowron greets George O'Donnell with a bases-clearing triple. The 9th is just a trip to the slaughterhouse, as nine runs cross the plate against Parnell and Jeffcoat, capped by a Skowron grand slam. It could be a coincidence, but Solly Hemus returns to the Clocker lineup in this game.

CLK 000 010 100 - 2 12 1
FLP 100 011 10x - 4 9 1
W-Feller L-Sullivan SV-Kinder
HRS: Kiner, Finigan
GWRBI-Fox

CLK 000 130 309 - 16 16 0
FLP 301 000 000 - 4 10 2
W-Brewer L-Dixon
HRS: Williams, Skowron
GWRBI-Williams

5/18: FLIPPIN' DUKE MEETS YOST WITH THE MOST

Some big creepy guy was across 2nd Avenue staring at the newsstand for like an hour yesterday. He looked familiar but it wasn't the big creepy guy who grabbed me by the collar at the Picadilly Hotel when Marilyn was in town and I snooped in on her. He was standing right in front of the little steamy wagon for Artie's Hot Franks, and in that hour he didn't buy even one hot frank, which isn't easy to do. Instead he smoked cigarettes, checked his watch a bunch of times and just stared at us. When he finally left I walked over and asked Artie if he knew who he was.

—"What do I look like? The Chamber of Commerce? I'm cookin' franks all day, kid. Eisenhower and his whole cabinet could be standing next to me and I wouldn't notice."

"Thanks Artie. Real helpful."

—"Anytime, kid. Want a foot-long? Extra relish no charge."

I shook my head, then saw that Pop was pacing around weirdly behind the register. I remembered he was listening to another Lagoons game and ran back across the street...

5/21: SHINY CHROME BUMPERS MOW DOWN COMMIES

After my stomach-churner of a flight back from the St. Louis dicecast, I was useless the next day, so Ma and Pop let me stay home and goof off for a change. It gave me a chance to follow the horse races on the radio from Yonkers, sneak a couple of Chesterfields on the fire escape, and also dig through Pop's special shoebox of baseball cards that he collected when the Hell's Angels played in the Bronx back in 1948.

They finished fourth in the Veeck Division at 75-87, a full 24 games behind the champion Phabulous Philcos that season, but he had Angels cards for five guys who are still playing this year: Vernon, Reese, Hodges, Snider, and Cavaretta. On the pitching side, he had cards for Rush, Brazle, Raschi and Garver too, though when I saw Vic Raschi's '48 stats (11-12 with a 3.42 E.R.A.) I knew the Clock Rockers would pay anything to have that kind of arm-work from him in '54. Pop also had cards for Hell's Benchers like Jimmy Outlaw, Johnny Blatnik, and Eddie Miksis, so I guess no collection is perfect. He told me he tried to swap a whole bunch of cards that year for a Stan Musial one, but no luck with that. Anyone who finished with a .391 average, 35 homers, 132 RBIs, a 1.160 OPS and 27 game-winners is gonna be a card that's hard to find, and compared to what he did for the Philcos, his performance for the Lagoons has been so weak by comparison I can't even bring Stan the Man's name up now around Pop. Good thing it's still early!

5/23: ENOUGH ALREADY WITH THIS MALARKEY

Bobby Z. had a date with a "neighborhood girl" set up for Saturday night and asked if I wanted to come along and take out her girlfriend Marge as a double date. I said okay, because what else did I have to do, but then he told me that HIS date was Bianca Ballorino, who I had a crummy time with myself less than a month ago! I balked and squirmed and balked some more and then he told me that this Marge doll had blonde hair and "tight hips". My Marilyn Monroe fantasy came back instantly, so I quickly gave in. At the least, I could pretend she was Marilyn…

5/24

Pretty dumb of me to schedule a double date for Saturday night when I have to fly back from Chicago the night before, right? Bobby Z. hasn't even told me what he's planning on us doing yet, but I know I'm going to be all plane-lagged and this Marge will be lucky if I'm awake enough to even smile in her direction. But that's the thing about nice dames: they tend to keep you awake regardless. Like the stewardess who brought me a whiskey and ginger over Indiana and then a pillow over Ohio and then a blanket over Pennsylvania…

5/25: BACK TO THE THRASHING BUSINESS

For the double date last night, Bobby Z. wanted to grab a few cheap wine bottles and head out to Coney Island. The amusement park doesn't open until Memorial Day (next week!) but sitting on the beach, gettin' stewed and possibly makin' out is always a gas. Unfortunately, Bianca and Marge had already decided on Brooklyn's Bay Ridge Roller Rink, and as usual, it was ladies first.

The problem was that I was more spazzy on roller skates than Mussolini would've been on a hockey rink, and as it turned out Bianca and Marge were both taking the Bay Ridge roller dancing class, so it only took fifteen seconds into the first Bill Haley song for me and Bobby to look like idiots. Marge was cute but hardly resembled Marilyn Monroe, so I told them I had a little fever and wobbily rolled over to the snack bar, where the Masters and Bikinis game out in Chicago was still going on a television, and it was tied 1-1 in the 6th. After a few relieved minutes with my vanilla Coke, Marge rolled up against my elbow, and her strong perfume nearly knocked me off the stool.

—"Don't you wanna skate with me, Paulie?"

"Did you see me out there? I stink!"

—"Everyone stinks at first. Don't you want me to teach you?"

It was a touch choice: tight ballgame, or skating lesson from a tight, perfumy doll. I glugged down the rest of my Coke and got off the stool…

5/26: THE MENACING FLIPS STRIKE AGAIN

There I was working the register yesterday, my mind enjoying memories of the perfumy kisses and groping I shared with

Marge Koshinsky last night in the back parking lot of the Bay Ridge Roller Rink, when Schnozzo decide to ruin my day.

—"Tell me your favorite movies, Paulie, and I'll tell you mine.'

"Kinda busy right now, Schnozz—"

—"Bomba the Jungle Boy with Johnny Sheffield, Neptune's Daughter with Red Skelton, Horatio Hornblower with Greg Peck of course, Abbott & Costello Meet the Invisible Man, oh yeah, Calamity Jane and Sam Bass with that dish Yvonne De-Carlo, HOO! Tell me your favorite girl actresses, Paulie, and I'll tell you mine."

I rang up two issues of National Geographic for a guy that had to be a local professor.

"Well...I guess I like Doris Day, and Audrey Hepburn—except she's a bit scrawny—"

—"WHAT?? No Marilyn? How can she not be at the top?"

I couldn't exactly tell him I had recently eaten lunch with her, so I said, "Marilyn's sexy and all, but not really my type." Which was also a mistake because then he tried selling me on her for the next ten minutes. I would have been shocked if Schnozzo didn't have a full-size poster of Miss Monroe over his bed in the Bronx.

FLIPSIDES 4, MENACE 3

Bob Feller and Carl Erskine are having a fine duel in frigid Milwaukee, with the Reds up 2-0 into the 8th, when post-trade hell breaks out. Former Menace Andy Seminick walks with one out, a wild pitch gets him to second, and with two gone, former Menace Gus Zernial bats for Feller and singles in Seminick. Then former Menace Eddie Yost (batting .400 since he left town) rips a triple to tie the game and tire out Erskine. Then Fox triples off former Flipsider Billy Hoeft. Then Duke Snider triples off Hoeft, their third straight three-bagger (they lead the league in those) before Art Fowler comes on and Groth pinch hits a lineout. Don Mossi then makes things ugly in the 9th, walking

four Reds for their third run but getting ex-Flipsider Jim Finigan to fly out with the bases loaded for his tenth save. Since the
Big Deal back on May 17th, the Flips are 9-1 and are suddenly
just a game behind the Clockers.

FLP 000 000 040 - 4 5 0
RED 000 101 001 - 3 6 1
W-Feller L-Erskine SV-Mossi

5/27: A ROLLER COASTER OF A HOLIDAY

It was hot and sticky for Coney Island's opening, and me and
Marge and Bobby Z. and Bianca had never seen such a mob.
Sure, it would've been more honorable to spend Memorial Day
thinking about our soldiers who bought the farm over in that
Korean war that ended last year, but heck, there were rides to
ride, a boardwalk to walk on, sea water to splash in and crazy
games to play!

The Cyclone roller coaster was our first stop, and Bobby
slipped the operator guy who he went to elementary school with
five bucks to get us into the front car. Marge had her eyes closed
for the whole ride so Bobby talked his friend into shooting us
through for a second one and threatened to make it a third if she
didn't open her eyes so Marge finally did and screamed in my
eardrum for the whole thing. Then it was a long line but worth it
at Nathan's Hot Dogs, then some makeout time on Deno's
Wonder Wheel. A lot of the game booths had portable radios
with ballgames going, so I caught snippets of the Masters,
Lagoons, and DiMaggios battles but none of the actual scores,
which bugged me.

Popcorn, candy apples and Italian ices were added to our
menus, and by the time we boarded the Cyclone for a third time,
Bobby Z. didn't look all that hot. He took the seat in front of us
with Bianca, then upchucked everything he ate on the first drop
and the wind blew the puke back over his hair and straight into
Marge's face! We spent the rest of the ride gagging and cursing,

and then half an hour getting cleaned up in the stuffy, packed restrooms. For that reason anyway, it was definitely a Memorial Day worth forgetting.

5/28: THE MAN IN THE SHINY BLUE SUIT

Ten minutes after the game ended in Baltimore last night, the goony big guy who was staring at me from the aisle found me at the exit gate and blocked my way.

—"Paulie Rubin?"

"Yeah. Who's askin'?"

—"Mr. DiMaggio wants to talk to you."

I was floored and speechless—but I spoke anyway.

"Seriously?"

—"Dead serious. This way."

"But I gotta catch the train back to New—"

—"You'll make the next one. Let's go."

So I followed him up two ramps and a rickety staircase into a special guest club box. Joe sat in a comfy chair with a perfect view of the Chrome Derbies field, where his Marilyn DiMaggios had just won again. He had on the sharpest and shiniest blue suit I'd ever seen, and smoked a cigarette with a cup of coffee in his hand.

—"Okay if I call you Paul? It happens to be my middle name."

"Uh, sure."

—"Jack Webb was nice enough to arrange this little meeting. See, we couldn't do it on the train because too many people would be bothering me, and besides we got another one to play here tomorrow."

"W-what's this about? I didn't mean to bump into you at Yonkers Raceway that day, I swear—"

—"Naw, forget that. I got a job for you, Paul. An important one."

"A job?? I already work for my pop at a newsstand."

—"Right. At Second and 84th. We know about that. Anyway,

something's gotta be done about these damn Masters of Suspense who are chewing up the division."

"Well…They happen to be real good."

—"No kidding. They've also been way too lucky, if you know what I mean."

"Um, not really—"

—"I want you to hang out at Rear Window Stadium since you live down the street from there. Like, whenever you can. This famous actress broad Grace Kelly they hired to be their hitting coach must be up to something, and I want her checked out."

"Up to what? And wouldn't it be easier if your, um…your wife looked into this? She might even know her!"

He flicked his cigarette ash. I could see some grey specks in his hair.

—"Mrs. DiMaggio is out in L.A. making another dumb movie. And she's none of your business. Naw, I want a smart kid like you no one will suspect. Did you know I used to hawk newspapers on the street in San Francisco when I was young? With Dario Lodigiani, who also made the bigs."

"That's neat…But um, how the heck am I supposed to do this spying thing?"

—"Your call, Paul. Along with…fifty bucks a week?"

It was awful tough to resist that. He stood up. He was pretty darn tall.

—"Listen. It's not even June yet and we're nine and a half back. I'm not used to losing."

And then Joltin' Joe walked over and put an arm around me.

"You'll do great, kid."

5/29:
ANOTHER CLOCKIN' GOOD TIME IN COONSKINVILLE

Pop was all full of spit and vinegar because his Lagoons had won two straight. Meanwhile, I was ringing up newspapers all day in a fuzzy fog because the Masters of Suspense and especially Grace Kelly were too much on my mind. They were due back in town on Friday after a day off to open a huge series with the Clock Rockers, with Joe's Marilyns also back and hosting the Red Menace at the Mr. Coffee Grounds. Meaning I would somehow need to spend tomorrow being a fifty bucks-a-week private dick.

Not that I was about to clue in Pop about it. I'd already fibbed that Donnie Gold had a sister with polio, and I was going to be spending a lot of time at the hospital with him visiting her.

—"That's nice of you, Paulie" he said, "But if we get a real busy day you may have to settle for a get well card."

5/30: THE EARL IS NO DUKE TODAY

It was cool and misty when I got up around eight in the morning. Ma was still asleep and Pop was in the shower. I threw on my leather jacket, hit Bedford Avenue and started walking south. Five or six blocks away, I could make out the looming light towers of Rear Window Stadium. A weird nervousness came over me, like I was that solicitor in the Dracula book sent to visit the evil Count at his castle.

Then I reached the ballpark, and saw the crowd at the ADVANCED TICKETS window. The Suspensers had taken the borough by storm in the last few weeks, and the line was snaking back and forth on the sidewalk and out into the street. An overweight stadium security guy was busy walking up and down the queue and chucking kids out of it that he saw cut in line.

—"Hey Paulie!" yelled a familiar voice, and I looked over to see Bobby Z. waving at me from the line. He was apparently buying some tickets for the big Clock Rockers weekend series, like nearly everyone else probably was.

"Hey. Thought you were a Mays and Bikini Bombs fan!"

—"I'm a baseball fan, man. Just like you. And the Masters are ruling it at the moment."

"Okay, listen. I got a favor to ask, and I'll make it up to ya big time…."

The favor was that I had him pretend to be cutting in line in front of me when the security guy turned in our direction. The second he did, I grabbed Bobby by the collar, shoved him out of the line and flagged down the security man.

"That's the fourth one I caught, mister! The way these crowds have been lining up, I bet you could use some extra help catching these punks, right?"

—"Well, yeah. If the club could afford it. You should see how many I nab trying to sneak through the gates after the game starts."

"See? That's what I'm talkin' about. Tell ya what, chief: You give me a little side job as an assistant security helper during the games and I'll do it for no pay at all the first couple weeks. I'm Paulie, by the way."

I put out my hand, He looked me over a long second, then put out his fat one and shook mine.

—"Charlie. But don't ever call me Chas. I hate that."

Charlie it was. And I took Bobby's place in line to get us both tickets for the opening game with a big grin on my face. I had found private access into the dark castle.

5/31: MANY TALES WITH SUDDEN ENDINGS

Holy cannoli, what a mob. I had nabbed upper deck grandstand seats just past third base, which Bobby Z. was more than grateful for, but getting up the ramps was like squeezing onto a Times Square subway car, and I swear there must have been five thousand standees along with the 31,902 folks packed into Rear Window Stadium. The Masters were 34-16 going in, nine games up on the Bikini Bombs, and everyone wanted a slice. I suppose there could've been some Clock Rocker fans on hand, but if so they were laying darn low.

Lefty Alex Kellner was facing righty Bob Rush, who'd won six straight after dropping his first two, and the joint went cuckoo bananas in the 2nd when Ray Katt put a two-run shot into the upper deck. The Clocks got one back in the 4th, but then Katt went clawing again. A Hofman walk, Renna single, and Ray's two-run triple off the "Luckies Taste Better" sign made it 5-1, knocked out Kellner, and I decided I needed to start looking for Grace Kelly.

—"You're going for another leak?" asked Bobby, "What'd you have? Beer for breakfast?"

"I can't tell you what I'm doing, Bobby. It's kind of a secret spy mission."

—"Okay, but now it's not secret anymore! You meeting a chick?"

"Maybe, yeah."

I spent the 5th and 6th innings scouting out the club level. Charlie expected me down below to watch a few of the entrance gates, and had given me a doinky little security badge to wear on my jacket, but I'd think of an excuse for him later. There was a whole row of private boxes just above the press box. One had its curtains drawn and I thought that could have been Alfred Hitchcock's, but he wasn't a big baseball fan even though he owned the club and I thought I'd read he was out in Bel-Air thinking about his next picture.

I moved through the stands, keeping my eye on the curtained box. I missed four more runs being scored on the field and when I glanced out at the scoreboard again, it was 7-3 Masters and the Clockers were on their third pitcher. Then I looked back up at the box and caught a glimpse of a sparkling ceiling light through the slot in the curtain. It was a chandelier.

That was good enough for me, and I wound my way behind the grandstand and used my badge to get myself up a guarded little ramp to the club level.

There was one box after another, their doors shut, all in a row. I crept along, counting them until the last one just past home plate, where I thought the chandelier was. Stopped when I saw a woman in an apron and carrying a tray of nail polish products exit the box. She left the door open a crack.

The crowd erupted in cheers down below, and I heard a guy say that Frank Thomas had just put one out. That made sense, seeing that Hank Sauer had been walked the last two times before him, the first time on purpose, and had made the White Hurt mad.

Anyway, I inched up to the suite's door. Took a peek inside and got a full four-second look at the divine creature who was Grace Kelly. She was laying on a little sofa against the wall, turned away from the curtained window overlooking the field. She seemed to have little interest in the game and was reading an *Argosy* magazine with one hand while holding her other hand aloft to dry her new nail polish. Marilyn Monroe was definitely the sexiest girl I'd ever met, but Grace was breathtaking on another level.

BAM! A big hand slammed the door shut behind me, and a six-foot ugly guy who was different from the six-foot ugly guy at Marilyn's hotel, yanked me away from it. I quickly held up my badge.

"Hold on! I'm working for Charley!"

—"I don't care if you're the King of Egypt. SCRAM!"

So I scrammed back down to join Bobby. And didn't miss much, game-wise. That thing was over the first time Ray Katt stepped to the plate, and I guess they'll be happy that the weather's about to heat up in Brooklyn.

6/1: CLOCK ROCKERS PEPPERED AND SHAKEN WITH MASTERFUL LONG BALLS

I had two problems at Rear Window Stadium for the second game. First, I wasn't going to get close to Grace Kelly's suite box because now there were TWO six-foot goons parked at the door, and second, Charlie was irked that I didn't show up at my post the day before and put me just inside the outfield bleacher gate to keep scofflaws from sneaking in. Luckily, there was a speaker box mounted nearby with Red Barber's play-by-play inside it.

I shoved away four or five neighborhood kids who tried to get in past me around the time of the first pitch from Chuck Stobbs, and with the game tied 1-1 after two, these two ducky boys in their 20s wearing Clock Rocker T-shirts and leather jackets who might have even traveled from Detroit tried to make their move and I thought that if I let them in, the crowd could disrupt things a little and maybe help the Brockton batters...

Nope. Them being there seemed to ignite the Clockers, as Schmitz doubled to start the 3rd, Michaels singled, Ted Williams (back from his latest injury) doubled, and Moose Skowron put one in the seats about five rows away! The visitors were up 5-1, the ducky boys hooted and hollered and got some beer thrown at them, and one Brooklyn fan yelled, "You watch, meatheads! This is only gonna make the Masters mad!"

And just like clockwork, they got mad. A Cass Michaels boot helped the Suspensers score three times in the bottom of the inning, and then home runs began peppering the seats around us. McDougald cranked one, then Bobby Hofman with a man on, and after a dinky Hoak single with Morgan on third, it was 8-7 Masters. Then, after hearing "SAU-ER! SAU-ER!" from the crowd every time he came up, Hank finally put one in orbit against Kemmerer in the 8th, the joint exploded, comeback win #21 was in the books, and the ducky boys slunk out of the bleachers and ballpark the way they came in.

Afterwards, all frustrated, I left past the players' parking lot. Recognized Sauer's big yellow Cadillac with its window open and got a storm in my brain. Two minutes later there was a note on his dashboard:

HEY HANK: RUMOR HAS IT YOUR HITTING
COACH HAS COMMIE CONNECTIONS.
—*YOUR BIGGEST CONCERNED FAN*

6/3: WHAT THE HECK DID I JUST DO?

Did one stinking note that I scrawled on a piece of paper in the Rear Window Stadium bathroom just turn over the baseball universe? If Sauer read it when he got home to his fancy house or apartment, then passed on the info to his Masters teammates that their lovely hitting coach could be a Communist spy, it would be the best explanation why yesterday's loss went the way it did.

6/4: THANKS AL ABER, FOR NOTHING

Okay, so maybe the Masters getting just two hits in their opener with the Big Flies had nothing to do with my note to Sauer. Joe Cunningham I guess was really sick with some infection I didn't want any details about, and maybe it was bothering the whole team, them being so closely knit and all. Either way, it was nice of the Clipper to show his appreciation for my note-leaving by buying a bunch of our Superman comics. I could picture him in his hotel suite at the Plaza, reading about Lex Luthor and toasting a cold one to his new employee Paulie—or Paul, as he put it. The Masters have one more with the Flies before hitting the road for Detroit (Clockers) and Baltimore (Chromers), so now I gotta think up some more creative spying while they're away.

6/5: DON'T GET LAGOONY ON ME, BABY

—"PAULIE! What's with all your disappearing lately? I've had to have Schnozzo help me out, and that's like having one of the Three Stooges. He short-changed four customers yesterday!"

"Sorry, Pop. But I told you. Donny Gold's sister—"

—"I don't wanna hear that no more. Your mother tells me Donny doesn't even HAVE a sister. You working some kind of side job or what?"

It was the moment of truth.

"Well…actually…I am. An old hero of yours asked me to do a few things for him."

—"What old hero? Max Baer? Snuffy Stirnweiss? Somebody

from the war—"

"Uh-uh. Joe DiMaggio."

I thought Pop's head was gonna fall off its neck. He pulled me behind the register and sat me down. It took me five minutes to explain everything to him, leaving out the part about trying to sabotage the Masters' pennant chances, of course. I told him I was getting Joe's suits pressed, getting his friends birthday gifts, placing horse bets for him at Yonkers, that sort of thing.

—"My God. You HAVE to invite the Clipper over for dinner. Your mother can bake him manicotti."

"I don't know about that, Pop. He's awful busy—"

—"Not too busy to meet one of his biggest fans? You know how many times Joe struck out in 1941, the year of his big streak? I happen to know. Thirteen."

This went on for another ten minutes, so I gave up trying to get out to Rear Window Stadium on the Masters' day off to see if Grace was rubbing ladies' bath oil on the team bats or some-thing. More than likely, she was at some fancy rich party out on a Hampton, yakking about fashion and clinking her wine glass.

6/7: HATS OFF TO FRED AS CLOCKERS ROCK ANOTHER ONE

Not easy to do a side spying job when your mark is in Detroit and you're stuck in Pittsburgh. The Lagoon/Blackboards game was a sad gas, and then I tried following some of the baseball writers around to some Steel City watering holes because I had a late train back.

That didn't work neither. No one knew who I was or wanted me along, so I shot a few racks of pool and lost twenty bucks for about an hour, then hung around Pittsburgh's old Union Station, which had a beautiful domed ceiling inside that looked like a lizard's eye. That seemed appropriate, seeing it's felt like various reptiles have been watching me all year...

CLOCKERS 4, MASTERS 3

A packed house at the Rock Shop for another series opener between the division leaders, and the Brocktonites even the season set at two games apiece by winning a tight thriller. A Ted Williams sact fly off Stobbs puts the Clocks ahead in the 1st, but Sauer's deep fly scores Hoak in the 3rd against Schmitz to tie it. A Skowron double after a single and walk in the 3rd makes it 2-1 Clockers but again the Masters knot it in the 5th on a booming Thomas double that also sees Sauer get nailed at home plate by Richie Ashburn! Bobby Hofman's solo blast one inning later makes it 3-2 Suspensers, but then a Campanella double and Logan triple tie it a third time. After Stobbs is pinch-hit for in the top of the 9th in a failed try to go back ahead, Clem Labine and his 1.50 E.R.A. come on for the last of the inning, but after Fondy pinch-hits and fouls out, Ashburn singles, gets to second on a passed ball, and Fred Hatfield bats for Michaels and rips a single into right to score the winner, making it five in a row for the Clockers and putting them eight over .500. Uh-oh...

MOS 001 011 000 - 3 6 0
CLK 101 001 001 - 4 10 0
W-Schmitz L-Labine
HR: Hofman
GWRBI-Hatfield

6/8: WE TOOK MANHATTANS, AND WISHED WE HADN'T

Back from Iron City Beer Town, I looked up Bobby Z. The Masters were still in Detroit, but the DiMaggios were at the Mr. Coffee Grounds to take on the Big Flies again. And I wanted to find a way for Bobby to meet Joe.

I had to tell Bobby about him, right? He was with me up at Yonkers that day we bumped into the Clipper, and now would be a good time to fill him in a bit. On the train out to the ballpark, I stuck with some of the same malarkey I had told Pop—about me running errands for Joe and picking up his suits and junk like that. No need to bring up the spying thing yet.

At the security gate I got the guard to call Joe upstairs and give him my name, and whoosh, up we went into a little private elevator. Bobby was impressed, and then we walked into Joe's private box. This thing was bigger than the whole Rubin apartment, and had a full bar and pool table. Joe greeted us in a different shiny suit and smoking a fresh cigarette. He arched an eyebrow at Bobby right away.

—"Who's this?"

"Bobby Zellman. My best buddy and he's um, really good at helping me run your errands." I gave Joe a little wink to make it clear Bobby didn't know any more.

—"Can I get you boys Manhattans?"

—"Uhh, I don't know," said Bobby, and I elbowed him in the ribs. "Sure, Mr. DiMaggio!" he cried.

—"Call me Joe, kid."

While his bartender made our drinks, we walked to a big glass window and looked out at the Coffee Grounds, where the Flies and Marilyns were limbering up. Three expensive cushy lounge chairs faced the field.

—"Sauer hasn't homered in a few days, and the Clockers took that opener against them in Detroit, so I like what you're—I mean, like the way things have been going lately, Paul"

"Yeah, no fooling."

Joe handed us our Manhattans and Bobby was so nervous and excited to be in Joe's presence that he downed the thing in one huge gulp, then choked and nearly fell over.

—"Slow but steady on those, kid. The same way I hit…Now where do you want your field box? First base side or third?"

"Huh?" I asked, glancing at the lounge chairs where I presumed he'd be joining us for the game.

—"Toots Shor and the Mayor are coming by for those, otherwise yeah." He reached into his suit pocket and took out a wad of tickets. "How about behind home?"

How could we say no?

6/9: CREATURE LAGOON FLOODS FORBES JUNGLE PARK

It was a slow summer day for the newsstand, so Pop decided to close it up for the time being and pay Schnozzo a few bucks to sit there on Sundays and keep the vagrants away.

I wish I had joined him. Five minutes into our cannoli and bagel brunch, four of Pop's buddies showed up to grill me about Joe DiMaggio.

—"Is he taller in person?"

—"Did he sign a bat for you?"

—"Why didn't he hit that ball past Ken Keltner in Cleveland and keep the streak going?"

And naturally…

—"Did you meet Marilyn Monroe yet?"

"What are ya, nuts?" I barked, "How could someone like me ever meet Marilyn Monroe??"

—"Bernie was just curious, Paulie," said Pop, defending his friend. "One week ago, who would imagine you'd ever meet Joe DiMaggio?"

He did have a point. Sometimes a guy just lives off his own crazy luck.

6/10: SAY IT'S SO, JOE

It was kind of a boring day, because all three New York clubs were out of town. Didn't feel like sitting around the newsstand all day hearing Schnozzo blab, so I called up Marge and took her bowling instead. Pop hardly noticed I took off early. He was still reelin' and a rockin' from the big 11-0 Lagoons win in Pittsburgh the day before, and Schnozzo was keeping him distracted with his idiocy.

Me and Marge bowled a few games at Kingpin Lanes and she wasn't too bad but I beat her twice, which was a lot more satisfying than my roller skating experience. We went for burgers and shakes afterwards, and she held my hand, and we cooed some sweet words back and forth across the table, and then she asked,

—"You think your friend Joe DiMaggio would ever go out with a Jewish girl?"

"First of all, he's married, and second, how the hell did you know he was my friend, which he really isn't?"

Turned out Bobby Z. had told Bianca, who of course had told Marge.

—"Also," she continued, "Married schmarried. Big celebrities like him date around left and right."

"Great, so call hm up. I gotta go home."

"Oh Paul-ie come on. I'm just joking."

"Yeah, well I'm not. The Lagoons are losing again and Pop's gonna need me to calm him down."

Thanks, Flipsides!

6/12: BASEBALL PLAYS THE MEN AGAIN

We interrupt your regularly scheduled Paulie shenanigans to bring you my detailed account of maybe the craziest ballgame so far this year—and that's sayin' plenty…

CLOCKERS 7, DiMAGGIOS 6 (13 innings)

It sure don't start that way. With Pollet facing Sullivan at the Rock Shop, the Clockers tally one in the 1st on two singles and a Skowron double, but the Mick puts a three-run shot in the upper deck in the 3rd and the Marilyns are suddenly thinking about a Detroit sweep. Two singles, a Sullivan sac and Ashburn triple ties it in the 4th, though, and then seven innings of scoreless frustration settle in for both teams. Sullivan retires 15 in a row at one point, then gets out of a few jams, while Pollet helps send it into extras by throwing five innings of one-hit ball.

Finally in the top of the 12th, Greengrass singles, Astroth walks, and with one out, Goodman singles in the go-ahead run. Mantle greets Hoyt Wilhelm with a sac fly to make it 5-3, and many Clocker fans start to head home. Big mistake. Wayne

Belardi, less dangerous with a glove than a bat, muffs an Ashburn grounder to start the last of the 12th. Michaels and Williams walk. Skowron beats out an infield hit which Belardi kicks
away for a second error and the game is tied again! New de facto
closer Howie Judson relieves Pollet and somehow gets Westlake,
pinch-hitter Courtney and Hemus to end the mess. Top of the
13th: With two outs, Furillo walks. MacMillan, who went in for
defense at shortstop, cracks a double to right with Furillo scoring
when Westlake boots the ball! 6-5 DiMaggios and any remain-
ing Clocker fans still in attendance begin to head home.

Wrong! Logan singles to start the last of the 13th, and after
one out, Ashburn walks, Michaels singles in another tying run
and Ted Williams singles to trot it off after going zero-for-five
in the game. The scary thing about the Clockers being seven
games over .500 is that Teddy Ballgame hasn't really begun to
hit yet.

MDM 003 000 000 002 1 - 6 10 2
CLK 100 200 000 002 2 - 7 15 1
W-Wilhelm L-Hudson
HR: Mantle
GWRBI-Williams

6/15: GRACE UNDER FIRE, SAUER POWER AIN'T ENOUGH

With my Grace-incriminating found note on Sauer's car suddenly headline material across the country, any problems I had
before getting near her private suite-box at Rear Window Stadium were now magnified a thousand. News reporters and not just
the daily baseball beat ones packed the hallways and ramps of
the place like crazy ants, and I actually had to spend the Masters
game against the Flipsides doing my security job at the bleacher
gate instead of trying to be Joe D's spy. From snatches of talk by
passing fans, reporters, and even from Charlie when he wasn't
getting on my case was that Grace was under fire but denying
any Commie involvement at all, and saying that "whoever would
create such a ghastly rumor about me needed to have his or head

examined." I was a little insulted by that, but still glad Sauer's hitting coach was rattled, and the result of the game yesterday gave me some hope…

6/16: FIVE BOROUGHS OF HAPPY DADS

Sorry, folks. No spying on Grace yesterday. No reservations made yet for Toots Shor's. Whitey Ford was pitching for the Lagoons down in Baltimore, so me and Mom made up a basket of brisket and prosciutto sandwiches, then found a shady spot by the water in Prospect Park for a Father's Day ballgame-on-the-radio picnic.

Pop knew most of the folks picnicking around us were Masters fans, but he didn't give a hoot, and cranked up the volume on his RCA transistor until Mel Allen's play-by-play drowned out the assorted Red Barber calls around us. The sandwiches and bottles of pop were yummy, and except for the five minutes when we had to go kamikaze on the tons of ants that were getting on our blanket, it was a great baseball holiday for all the dads in the park—even for any stray DiMaggios fans. And when Ford completed his second straight shutout and the fourth straight win for the Lagoons, often shy Pop leaped in the air, scattered some of his potato chips, and yelled "THAT'S A WHITEYWASH! HOW ABOUT THAT!"

6/17: MAYS, BIKINIS FLIP THE SCRIPT ON FLIPSIDES

Senator McCarthy's new hearing was all over the radio on Monday, and we probably did half the business we normally do at the newsstand. When it began at 10 a.m. over WCBS, people began to pause and listen when they wandered by and we had to tell them to stop clogging the sidewalk. Even Bobby Z. and Donny Gold came over to console each other and fantasize about Grace when she finally entered the hearing room.

—"This is just just sad." said Bobby.

—"What's sad is that isn't being broadcast on television,"

said Donny.

—"I'm trying to imagine what she's wearing…"

There was a long silent pause, then Donny looked at him.

—"Short skirt, low-cut blouse, and velvet gloves?"

—"Same here."

Most of the hearing was a bunch of boring legal talk, until McCarthy suddenly droned that "I'm in possession here of a piece of note paper, given in secret to Masters of Suspense ballplayer Henry John Sauer following a game, that incriminates team hitting instructor Miss Kelly as being a member of the Communist Party. How do you answer for this, Miss Kelly?"

The crowd hushed but we didn't hear a peep from her. Then some attorney on her side said, "Given the seriousness of the charge and flimsy nature of the so-called evidence you possess, Miss Kelly has chosen not to dignify this hearing with an answer."

Bobby and Donny broke into giddy laughter and elbowed me.

"—They got nothing on her! Bet McCarthy wrote that note himself, right Paulie?"

I nodded and nodded and then ran to find a bathroom.

6/19: HOME INVASION AT OZZIE & HARRIET'S

Bobby Z. took the night train back from Chicago, but he still showed up at the newsstand just after 9:30 in the morning with a crazed look in his eyes.

—"Grace is making a statement in half an hour and it's on television!"

I put Schnozzo at the register and we hopped on a subway to lower Manhattan, where the former "Radio Row" was now dominated by TV stores. Three on one block had the hearing going out on the sidewalk, and we joined a gaggle of pedestrians around the first big Philco we came to.

Grace was so stunning, and just about glided through the

hearing room to her seat, wearing a completely different short skirt and low-cut blouse, this one topped by a necklace of big pearls. Bobby was so entranced he could barely breathe.

—"Thank you, Senator McCarthy," she began, with a voice that could melt margarine. "I have listened to your two days of creative lies, and I must say I find them comical and so, so unnecessary. It is far more likely that this' scandalous' note left in Mr. Sauer's auto was written by a jealous Black Lagoons Matter fan. Because I am more of a true-blooded American than you will ever be, Senator. What kind of cheese did your mother feed you back in Wisconsin? Have you really nothing better to do than ruin good people's reputations day in and day out? You strike me as little more than a weak and wicked man without a shred of decency and frankly, you should be ashamed of yourself! Now if you'll all excuse me, I have a professional first place ball team to attend to."

She picked up her white purse and glided out of the hearing room with her lawyers in tow. The crowd around us on the sidewalk roared in triumph, and McCarthy looked like a teacher had just paddled his bottom. For the moment at least, my spying career had been happily put on hold.

6/20:
HOWIE IS ZOWIE, MARILYNS ARE MUG MASTERS

I went to a used bookstore in Times Square on my lunch break and bought a handful of sleazy paperback spy novels, like "Agent of the Devil", "Murder is My Business", and "Think Fast, Mr. Moto", then spent the rest of the day sneaking in paragraphs while I worked. No new ideas for putting the whammy on the Masters jumped out at me, and with Grace telling off that creepy dope McCarthy at the hearing, I figured the Masters clubhouse was tighter than ever. Though that didn't explain what happened at the Mr. Coffee Grounds yesterday…

Home of 1954 Freaks League Baseball

OZZIE & HARRIET DIVISION			
Clock Rockers	38	31	—
Blackboard Seven	37	34	2
Chrome Derbies	35	36	4
Flipsides	34	35	4
Red Menace	33	37	5
Lord of Big Flies	29	37	7.5

RICKY & LUCY DIVISION			
Suspense Masters	44	25	—
Marilyn DiMaggios	34	32	8.5
Bikini Bombs	33	34	10
K2 Summiteers	32	34	10.5
Coonskin Caps	30	36	12.5
B. Lagoons Matter	29	38	14

GET SET
for Summer!

CHAMPION

GAMES OF THURSDAY, JUNE 20TH

	MOS	7
	MDM	14

	BKB	5
	K2S	6

★Star of the Day★
HOWIE POLLET

DiMAGGIOS 14, MASTERS 7

In a wildly entertaining football game, Howie Pollet spots the Masters two early field goals before Chuck Stobbs gets blitzed in the 4th, and the DiMags send a dozen men to the plate for eight runs and outscore the Suspensers 14-1 the rest of the game. Granny Hamner doubles three times, Rosen goes 3-for-4 and knocks in three, but Pollet is the true hero, whacking four singles and scoring all four times, and throwing a 3-hitter at the Masters after the 2nd inning. The win puts the second place Marilyns just seven back in the loss column, with Garcia facing Art Houtteman in to-day's game.

MOS 420 001 000 - 7 6 1
MDM 008 130 20x - 14 17 1
W-Pollet L-Stobbs
HR: Greengrass
GWRBI-Hamner

6/22: DOING THE TOWN WITH JOE
FOR THE WRONG REASONS

—"I really like you Paulie," said the Clipper after our third Manhattan at Toots Shor's sometime last night, "Can I call you Paulie?"

"Sure! Trying to remember why you've been calling me Paul."

—"Cause that's my middle name, and you remind me of me. Didja know I used to hawk papers like you when I was a kid?"

"Yeah Joe, you told me that already."

And so that went. What started out as him just buying us dinner at Toots got awful boozy awful quick, because the Masters put a double-hurt on his ball team that afternoon and he was getting all apologetic for giving me what looks more and more like an impossible side spying job. My brilliant plan of writing the infamous "Commie note" to Sauer just blew up, and his teammates apparently rallied to Grace Kelly's cause. Toots and his usual cronies at the restaurant were thrilled to see him anyway, where he was either called "Big Dago" or "the Daig" right and left, and Frank Sinatra even stopped by the table with some goofy redhead to whisper something sinister in the Daig's ear.

Anyway, after yummy Lobster Newburg and a few more drinks, my stomach was gurgling and the night was spinning. Next thing I remember was his driver taking us a bunch of miles out to Long Island, with Joe all sloshed, lighting cig after cig and whining about his famous wife.

—"We don't get along too well anymore, y'know…I love the hell outta Marilyn, but I just want her on my arm all the damn time and these movie jerks got her coming and going and dressing her up in these slutty outfits. Its awful, Paulie."

I nodded, then sort of passed out, and the next thing I knew it was morning, and I found myself lying on the huge green front lawn of some seaside house. And Joe and his driver were nowhere to be seen. A Japanese gardener walked over and kicked me in the shin.

—"You no sleep here!"

"Huh? Okay, sorry....S-sleep where?"

—"You no sleep on Grace Kelly's grass!"

6/23: WHEN THE ROCK SHOP BECOMES WESTLAKE VILLAGE

Okay, maybe the Clipper was as skunked as I was when he told his driver to pull me out of the car and dump me on Grace Kelly's lawn, but I think he was trying to tell me something. Like, do your stupid job. So after the gardener booted me off her massive property overlooking South Oyster Bay, I doubled back and found a way to loop around to the rear of the glass-windowed house and peek through a wooden fence at the pool area. I was beyond groggy and needed a big cup of coffee poured on my head, but the sea air kept me awake and I waited an hour until Grace stepped out her sliding door in a snappy yellow swimsuit, put on a matching cap and dove into the Olympic-sized pool.

After a number of laps a butler brought a telephone out on a serving tray along with a glass of orange juice, and she took the call on a lounge chair close enough for me to almost make out her words.

—"Yes Hank," she purred, "Bob can be tough, but so can you, and you know it…Well, sometimes he likes to throw a big curve with his first pitch, so you need to be ready for that, okay?… No, I won't make batting practice today, but I'll be seated behind your dugout with my field glasses as always, and wearing…oh, a blue hat this time. As always, darling…As always."

She hung up the phone, sipped her juice and dried herself off with a terrycloth towel. I slunk back off the property, my mind whirling. "Bob" had to be Porterfield, who was starting for the DiMaggios that afternoon, but what in heck was this "darling" stuff? Was Big Hank getting extra after-ballgame attention?

6/25: IT'S A GRAND SLAMMER JAMMER!

Marge was back in the picture all of a sudden. She had to write a paper for the night class she was taking in U.S. History, and because I was a baseball nut she figured I knew a little more than most about the "Commie Note" to Hank Sauer that got his famous and beautiful hitting coach in brief trouble with the feds.

I lied of course and told Marge I knew as much about it as she did, but she invited me over to her apartment anyway to help her type something up. Turned out that her roommate was conveniently out of town, Marge had conveniently baked some lasagna and also conveniently bought a bottle of good red wine.

So I think we got maybe one paragraph written.

6/26: LONG DISTANCE BOMBS APLENTY

I showed up at the newsstand twenty minutes late this morning with a saucy hangover and Marge-smell all over me. "Sheesh," said Pop, "Get some coffee and throw it in your face. You look like some cockamamie hoodlum." Schnozzo was annoying me most of the day too, so it was a relief to go run an errand for Joe on my lunch hour, which involved dropping his favorite suit off at his favorite dry cleaner in Chinatown. I went to the wrong address twice and the wrong Mr. Li once, and by the time I got back to the stand the afternoon newspaper editions were already dropping and I had to work double-time to get all the bundles cut open.

That was when Pop told me I had a long distance phone call through some operator. I grabbed the phone and walked it to the back corner of the stand where I could maybe hear the person.

—"Is this Paulie Rubin?" said the operator.

"Yup."

—"Go ahead, miss."

The voice was cheery and breathy and I instantly recognized it.

—"Hi Paulie! It's Marilyn!"

"Oh hey! Hello—"

—"I just wanted to tell you that there's a week-long break on my picture so I'm flying back to New York for a couple of days to work with my voice coach Hal Schaefer—he's my other coach. But no one can know about this trip, especially Joe, so because you were such a sweetie to me when we met last time I was wondering if you could drive me around a bit while I'm there and keep me away from all those reporters. You know, like my private escort?"

"Uhhhh…"

—"Don't worry. I'll disguise myself again. And I'll make it worth your while."

—"Paulie!" yelled Pop, "Where'd you put the *Herald Tribunes*??"

"Ummm, sure I guess—"

—"Great! So I'll call you in a couple days when I know when my flight arrives?"

"Uhhhh…okay."

I didn't remember where I put those *Herald Tribunes*. Or how to breathe.

6/28: HELLO, AUNTIE JEAN

The guy I rented the green Chevy Bel-Air from was way too nosy, so thankfully he believed me when I said my aunt was coming to town to be driven around and I needed a comfortable car. I raced out to La Guardia Airport in the heat of afternoon traffic, parked the thing and got inside the terminal wearing my phony chaueffer cap a minute before the plane from Los Angeles arrived. The sign I was holding up said JEAN NORMAN and as the passengers came off the plane and walked past me, I started nervously looking everywhere for Marilyn.

Then soft fingers tapped my shoulder from behind, and this slightly stooped old woman with grey hair, a black dress and black veil over her face stood there. She also had a familiar whispery voice.

—"Hi Paulie. Aunt Jean's ready when you are!"

I grabbed her suitcase and quickly walked us out of the terminal.

First place I drove her was back to the Picadilly Hotel in Times Square, where she always stayed on her "secret" trips to New York, and where she was meeting voice coach Hal Schaefer later. After I did the checking-in part for her at the desk, saying "my aunt needs a super quiet room because she's in mourning over her husband," I brought her up to her room on the 15th floor, where the first thing Marilyn did was pull off her old lady wig, throw open her suitcase, fish out casual slacks and a blouse and hop into the bathroom for a shower.

I quickly called Pop at the newsstand to see how things were going and he was all excited because "the Clipper called for you!" Oh great. Seems that a button was missing from the suit he got back from that dry cleaners in Chinatown and I needed to get down there before they closed and raise holy hell with them. Meanwhile Marilyn came out of the shower in a flimsy robe with her hair all wet and I suddenly had no idea what the hell I was going to do.

—"I am so famished for a Waldorf salad, Paulie honey," she said, "Could you see if they have one downstairs while I dress?"

The good news was that Joe was far away in Chicago watching his DiMaggios play. The bad news was everything else...

6/30: GUESS WHO CAME TO DINNER

After 48 hours of madcap logisticals and ruination to my brain and heart, she finally flew the New York coop this morning. I think I get why Joe loves her and she drives him nuts.

I had kept my "dinner guest" identity a secret until a minute before she walked into our Brooklyn apartment. Marilyn had shed her old lady disguise for a good try at looking like a normal girl-next-door—if the place next door happened to be Park Avenue. She wore a white cashmere sweater over a dark blue hoop skirt, and looked so downright Marilyn it was hard to mistake her for anyone else. So I kept her outside on the landing while I prepared Pop at the door.

"I know you'll think this is nuts, but just bear with me a sec, Pop."

—"Too late. We already think you're nuts."

"Okay, but take a big breath, and remember how tough it was to believe I'd met Joe DiMaggio like a couple of weeks ago."

—"Is Joe out there? Did you bring him to Flatbush?"

"No, Pop. He's still in Chicago another day. So instead...I brought his wife."

I stepped aside, ushered Marilyn through the door and my parents simultaneously swallowed their tongues.

—"Hi Mr. and Mrs. Paulie!" she cried with a saucy little dip of her bottom, "Thanks for inviting me!"

—"C-call me Sid."

—"Paulina...Pascatore...Rubin."

The moment the shock wore off, Pop, wearing his trademark sleeveless undershirt like he always did at home, excused himself and ran down the hall, while Mom began changing the look of the dinner table, swapping out the plates for her best china and finding a vase of flowers to stick there. By the time I had walked Marilyn to Pop's collection of albums to pick something out for the record player and filled Mom in about the star's secret visit to New York and our first meeting over a month ago, her "Meatballs Paulina" was ready on the stove. Pop had changed into his best suit and loudest tie, and then embarrassed me and bothered Mom further when he pulled back Marilyn's chair and insisted on helping tuck in her napkin-bib over her white sweater.

—"Sidney! She can do that herself!"

Marilyn was as delightful as she could be, considering how much red wine she drank, and Mom kept asking suggestive questions about her "friendship" with me, and with the same

Benny Goodman record still playing after dinner, the four of us danced a bit in the living room, me, Pop and Mom taking turns spinning with Marilyn. The phone rang around eight and I ran to answer it and yanked the cord around the corner because I had a sense of who it was.

—"Hey Paul. Find anything?"

"Sorry, Joe. If she was in town I'd know because it would be all over the local papers with photos and crap—"

—"Whaddya sorry about? If she was in New York without telling me, then SHE'D be the one who's sorry. I gotta keep tabs on this girl every second."

Marlyn giggled loudly in the other room.

—"What was that?"

"Oh, just one of our goofy neighbors. My mom likes to have people over when she makes her special meatballs."

"Well, slip me that recipe sometime and I'll give ya another ten. Anyway, look forward to seeing you at those games of ours against the Masters this week. Hope you got a new idea planned, 'cause we sure as hell need one."

I hung up and re-joined the party. Marilyn was stumbling around a bit too much and yelling funny things out the window and neighbors were getting too curious, so I let Pop give her a long goodbye hug that I practically had to pry open with a crow-bar, and rushed her back into my rented Bel-Air.

I ordered her an early taxi to take her back to LaGuardia, and at her hotel room door made her promise to wear her old lady disguise again for the flight. She nodded and grinned and plant-ed a long and very real kiss on my mouth.

—"You're the best, Paulie…Just a great…romantic helper." She just about fell into her room. I could've helped her get into bed and all, but something stopped me. Like valuing my life.

7/1: BREAK TIME

Is there such thing as a celebrity escort hangover? Well, I had one yesterday, and thankfully there were no games being played in town and Pop gave me the day off. He was still humming "Stompin' at the Savoy" at breakfast and no doubt daydreaming about his famous living room dance partner. My plan was to grab a bus to Sheepshead Bay and just stare at the water for a while, but that's when Marge called and wanted to go feed the ducks in Central Park. So we met at a well-known hot dog wagon on 5th and East 79th and asked for an extra plain roll.

The ducks didn't seem to be around, but pigeons were every-where so we found a bench in the shade and let them swarm us.

"Ya gotta spread the bread crumbs around," I told her. "If one bird eats too much it could explode right in front of us."

—"That's crazy, Paulie. Where'd you hear that?"

"Trust me. I've seen it happen."

She poked my ribs, then snuggled up next to me. Then noticed something on the collar of my leather jacket and picked it off.

—"What's this?"

"Huh?"

She was holding a long piece of blonde hair between her fin-gers. It was definitely not hers.

—"It's someone's hair, Paulie."

"Yeah, it's yours. So what?"

—"Mine is sandy blonde". She pointed at her head. "This is almost white, and it definitely isn't mine."

"Cripes, Marge. Maybe I brushed up against some girl on the subway, I don't know."

—"You sit that close to people on the subway?"

I sighed in exasperation, started chucking bread pieces at the same fat pigeon as fast as I could.

—"What's the matter with you? You said they'd explode!"

"Hell, I'm gonna explode if you stay on me about this piece of hair!"

—"I couldn't reach you for almost two days, Paulie. How do I know what you've been doing or who you've been seeing?"

"Gee-zus…"

—"For all I know you're back with Bianca!"

"Her hair's dark."

—"Or another friend of hers who's blonde! You're asking me to trust you but how can I do that?"

"I was saying to trust me about the pigeons."

She snatched what was left of the hot dog bun from my hand and mushed it on the side of my head.

—"You creep! I can't go with someone who won't take me seriously, Paulie Rubin. Enjoy your exploding birds."

And she grabbed her bag and marched away. Every hungry pigeon in the park seemed to be at the bench now, and I sat and just stared at them as they swarmed over my ankles.

7/2: FIVE THRILLERS FOR THE PRICE OF NONE

It was killing me to be stuck in Cincinnati on dicecast duty yesterday while the DiMaggios were opening a huge four-game series in Brooklyn with the Masters—which will include a Fourth of July doubleheader. But Joe was okay with me sending Bobby Z. to Rear Window Stadium as my "spying assistant", even though he still didn't have a clue why he was supposed to keep his ears and eyes open for "possible subterfuge", as I put it. I arranged to talk to him twice on pay phones during their game, once after the 3rd inning and once after the 6th, but each time was kind of useless.

"What's going on?"

—"Nothing yet, Paulie. Lemon and Wehmeier are both throwing goose eggs."

"What's Sauer done?"

—"Grounded out in the 2nd. Thomas and Cunningham then singled but Lemon stranded 'em both."

"Okay, call me at the same number after the 6th."

I paced around my Cincy hotel room for 45 minutes. The game at Crosley Crush wasn't until 6:30 p.m.

"—Sorry, Paulie. Still no score. Lemon and Wehmeier look like Cy Johnsons out there."

"This is bad. The Masters win on late homers all the time. Every time Sauer and Thomas come up, get down near the on-deck circle somehow and start ribbing them."

—"What do I say?"

"How should I know? Make something up!"

I never heard from Bobby again, until he called me from a nearby Brooklyn precinct after the game, where Masters fans beat him up and he was tossed out of the park and arrested for being a public menace. At least the game turned out the way we wanted…

7/3: MASTER OF DISGUISE VISITS THE MASTERS

Joe's big town car rolled up to the newsstand at 12 noon like he promised.

—"Wow. Who the heck is that?" asked Schnozzo.

"Mind your own business," I said, and slipped into the back seat. Joe was crabby already because Grace Kelly had a bee in her head scarf over the Masters dropping the opener the day before, and didn't want him anywhere near any of the private boxes for the second game.

—"Grace is a real stuck-up tomato sometimes," he said, "I think we'll drop you off at the gate and listen to the game in the parking lot."

I told him no stinkin' way was that happening, and told his driver to stop at a thrift store on the way.

Forty-five minutes later, we had paid through the nose for scalped box seats and Joe walked right in and sat beside me—a little warm inside his wrinkled used slacks, bulky sweater, dark glasses, fake beard and cab driver hat.

"You better keep me hydrated with lemonades, Paul." he whispered. After his first one, his spirits picked right up because the DiMaggios scored three times off lousy Chuck Stobbs in the

3rd, starting with a bad omen when no-hitting Roy McMillan got plunked. A Porterfield bunt followed, then Goodman singled in the first Marilyns run, Hamner doubled, and Al Rosen singled in two more. Stobbs was gone for good one lemonade later when Furillo opened with a line single to right that Sauer butchered to get him to third. Crandall and McMillan singled, Porterfield tripled, and Clem Labine took over as the crowd booed Stobbs off the mound. It didn't get any better for the home folks and I could hear Joe giggling off and on in between his lemonades and cigarettes. The DiMags ended up winning by seven runs, the Masters were hardly masterful with their gloves, booting four balls, and when I escorted Joe to the packed men's room later so he could take a very long leak, he leaned into my ear.

—"Love what you've been doing for me, Paul," he said. "We got them spooked and we're riding up the ladder on those Bikini tails."

"I didn't do crap today, Joe."

—"Well, let's pretend you did. Prime rib and drinks at Toots Shor's are my treat tonight."

"Okay, but no dumping me at Grace Kelly's house again please."

7/4: FIREWORKS OF ALL KINDS

An overflow holiday doubleheader mob was expected at Rear Window Stadium, so there was no way I could evade Charley as far as my security duties went at the bleacher gate. With the DiMaggios taking the first two games of the series, there was a whole slew of their fans trying to worm their way into the park on top of the usual Suspenser scofflaws, and four or five times I had to help break up fights between the two gangs either just outside or inside the gate. With Houtteman and Garcia locked in a scoreless duel the first three innings of the opener, I wasn't missing much, but then I heard the bleacher crowd roaring and snuck up an aisle to watch some of the bottom of the 4th—

which was all I needed. Morgan singled, Bell tripled, and after
Red Wilson whiffed. Sauer singled, White Hurt Thomas put one
in the cheap seats, Cunningham tripled, McDougald hit a sac fly,
and the five runs that decided the game were in.

Between contests I cruised around the park looking for Joe
in his old man outfit to no luck, and figured he was telling the
truth when he said he might play some golf with Toots instead.
Anyway, after kicking out a second round of no-ticket inter-
lopers, the nightcap began as another scoreless duel, this time
between spot men Gordon Jones and Jim McDonald. Gordon
was the one who had the goods, though, and I left my post for
the top of the 6th, when Mantle bashed a leadoff homer, Goodman doubled, and after one out, Dropo singled, Hamner tripled,
Furillo doubled and a wild pitch made it 4-0 Marilyns. Charley
then tracked me down with a volcanic face because a half dozen
DiMaggio fans had gotten through the bleacher gate.

"What the hell am I paying you for?" he yelled at me in front
of everyone, "Gimme your security cap and badge and get the
hell out of here!" So much for that way into the park, right? I left
through the same gate, snuck around to the first base grandstand
and slipped back in over there, in time to watch the DiMaggios
tack on another four-spot in the 9th for a Gordon Jones shutout
and three out of four in the enemy park!

With one out to go in the game, I was in a wise-ass kind of
mood, and had weasled my way down to one of the empty and
expensive box seats behind the Masters dugout. Red Wilson was
their last hope, and he suddenly sliced a wicked foul liner right
toward my section. The ball was an inch away from whacking
a little girl in a Masters cap sitting beside me but I lunged out
and snagged the thing with my bare hand at the last second! The
crowd applauded, I handed the souvenir to the girl, got embraced
by her grateful parents, and after Wilson whiffed and the crowd
began filing out, the next thing I knew the head usher was running down the aisle to block my path.

"You the guy who made that foul catch?"

"Uhh...yeah."

"Thought so. Miss Kelly would like to meet you in her private suite-box."

Gotta get to those holiday recaps now, folks. Meaning I'll tell ya about that amazing business tomorrow.

7/5: MEETING WITH AMAZING GRACE

Grace Kelly was more breathtaking in person than I could have dreamed. Even the way she wrinkled her nose was sexy, let alone the pleated red skirt that swished when she crossed her lavish suite box to shake my hand.

—"They tell me your name is Paulie Rubin."

"That's right, ma'm."

—"Mmm. That won't do. You'll be calling me Grace from now on."

"Er...from now on?"

—"Yes of course. That young girl who's life you just saved with that heroic foul ball catch happens to be the daughter of one of our wealthiest season ticket holders! How could I not reward you by hiring you to be our new team ball boy? Or should I call you 'ball man'?

"Gee-zus. That's sure swell and all. But I work for my pop at his newsstand in the city—"

—"Oh fiddlesticks. He'll understand. Even though we're still in first place, we've been in a frightful slump of late and we could desperately use a good luck charm to join the club. Why, I've been told that ball teams in the earlier days of the century employed human mascots—either a child or a hunchback dwarf—for just this purpose!"

"Gee, thanks..."

—"Regardless, those Communists from Milwaukee who I swear I have nothing to do with are here to play us tomorrow, and I expect you to report for ball man duty by the second game at the latest, so you can meet all of our handsome muscular fellows."

I refrained from telling Grace that Pop was a big Lagoons fan, and at dinner that night, news of my new job didn't go over too well.

—"This means you'll be on the road with those creeps all summer! Who's going to help me at the newsstand, I ask you?"

"I'm sure Grace can find someone. And can't you just put Schnozzo more in charge?"

—"You kidding? I'd rather put a smelly hobo from Hoboken in charge!"

It was certainly a tough decision for me, but I also knew that Clipper Joe might help Pop out somehow—seeing that his "spy" was now gonna be inside the enemy clubhouse.

7/6: INTO THE LIONS DEN, FOR BETTER OR WORSE

Grace may have only been the Masters' hitting coach, but judging by the way she was treated around the ballpark and the quickness with which the team clubhouse parted when she escorted me inside it, she was a lot closer to glamorous royalty. Players went stone quiet, quickly covered themselves if they were still in underwear, and looked me up and down like I was some kind of prince for just being at her side.

—"Meet Paulie, everyone!" she announced, "He'll be our new ball man, and lives in the neighborhood just a few blocks away from here apparently. Paulie will help us out on the field gathering our most treasured, non-bat equipment. Treat him like the nice little brother you may or may not have had, and I'm sure he'll be a great addition to the team."

She floated back out and left me standing there, and I was too nervous to even look up. Stingbean, their 280-pound equipment manager who was shorter than me, walked up and handed me a Masters cap and fluffy new uniform with the number 97 on the back. Showed me to a tiny locker in the corner next to bench man Jim Brideweser's, and I quickly changed into it while assorted players strolled by to give me obligatory hand shakes or pats on the back. Joe Cunningham and Gil McDougald were real friendly. I thanked Red Wilson for lining that foul ball that I caught and he snickered. Mike Garcia slipped me a matchbook from some place called the Hide-a-Way Jungle Room in Newark.

—"Never bought into this mascot thing," said Frank Thomas, a big guy with big ears, crewcut, and crazy eyes, "So bring us more good luck, 97, or I'll barbeque your behind."

Slugger Hank Sauer never introduced himself at all, probably because local reporters had him cornered at the far end of the room, but I was okay with that. If Hank ever found out I was the one who wrote the famous "Commie note" and dropped it in his car that day, I'd have a Louisville Slugger re-arranging my brain in no time.

MASTERS 4, MENACE 0

It was fun collecting the balls from the umpire and scooting after stray foul ones near home plate, but other than that the team didn't need my help, as Don Liddle hoodwinked the punchless Menace on five scattered hits and they got to Art Fowler for a pair of two-run innings mid-game on flurries of walks, singles, and doubles. Being more up close to the Masters, I was amazed how great they got along in the dugout, and even had time to chuck sunflower seeds and peanut shells at my head while I kneeled on the field between batters.

RED 000 000 000 - 0 5 1
MOS 000 220 00x - 4 8 0
W-Liddle L-Fowler
GWRBI-Hoak

7/8: THE SCARY BIG GUY HAS SCARIER FRIENDS

Hank Sauer was chewing some tobacco on the dugout bench when I slid in beside him. He was tall, with huge arms and a big nose (teammates called him "the Honker"), but apparently didn't fancy himself a clubhouse leader, even though he was leading them in almost all offensive categories when Grace assigned me to try and relax him.

—"Yeah, kid. I know. I've been in plenty of slumps." He rubbed one of his big hands on my head. "I'll try this anyway, even though I know it won't help. Only way to get out of a downslide is to have faith and work your way out of it."

I told him that's how my life had been so far, struggling to make money with my Pop and all, and he understood. Told me about growing up a Pirates fan with his brothers in Pittsburgh and rooting for Pie Traynor and Arky Vaughn and others, and his two years with the Coast Guard during the War.

—"Did my duty for the country then, so when that note about Miss Kelly's Commie connection fell in my lap, I had to bring it to Washington, right? She's been cool to me ever since around the batting cage, so maybe that hasn't helped." He squeezed his fingers around the handle of the 41-ounce bat in his hand. "I swear, if I ever find the lowlife who wrote that note—"

I nervously nodded and told him I had to go collect the game balls and hopped out of the dugout. Then noticed that creepy Frank Thomas and his spittin' pal Joe Cunningham had been watching our little talk. And they didn't look too pleased.

7/9: LIKE I NEED THIS AGGRAVATION

Bad enough I got every Masters hitter except Frank Thomas rubbing things on my head before each game. Now I had to deal with the Blackboard Seven's annoying ballboy. Apparently the visiting players caught wind of my "lucky mascot" role and unleashed Delby, a pimply, nasty delinquent who couldn't have been older than sixteen who tried to pick at least three fights with me during yesterday's game. Every time I collected an armload of balls from down the line or the end of the dugout or brought three or four new ones out to the home plate ump,

Delby would block my way with his rat eyes, cigarette breath and BBS cap perched on top of his junior ducktail.

—"Those balls are OURS."

"The hell they are."

—"Stop taking our balls or I'll tell your boss."

"You're gonna tell Grace Kelly? Have fun trying that."

—"Well, she's a no-good Commie spy and her pictures stink. And you're stealing our balls."

"How about I just get Sauer's bat and smash YOUR balls?"

And so it went for an hour and a half. I get that the Black-boards are a little angry with how their team is faring in Brook-lyn, but gimme a break with this. I really thought Sauer socking his 37th homer with two aboard in the 3rd off Bob Chakales would shut Delby up, but it only made him worse.

—"Hey dork!" he yelled from the top step of the Blackboards dugout as the top of the 7th began for another frustrating inning against Bob Rush, "Meet me outside the players gate after the game so I can pound your face!"

"It's a date!" I yelled back. Rush polished them off for the 56th Masters win not long after that, which was good because I knew certain people would be in a cocky mood. When I walked out of the park after the game there was Delby near their team bus, now wearing a black leather jacket over his scrawny body and chomping some gum with a cigarette behind his ear.

—"Ready to cry, dork?"

"You tell me first," I replied. As Frank Thomas, Joe Cunning-ham, and Red Wilson stepped out of the shadows behind me in street clothes and rolled up their sleeves. Delby swallowed his gum, turned white, and slithered onto their bus like the rat that he was.

7/11: ONE FOR THE ROAD, AND HOW!

There was only one ballgame to follow the details of yesterday, and that was a blessing and a half. It was so hot and sticky while

I waited for the Masters team to arrive in St.Louis that I forgot how many times I changed my shirt. The hotel room I was stuck in had a broken air conditioner, and the dinky fan they gave me barely rustled my hair. So I spent part of the day with my feet in the water at Carondelet Park, and the rest of it sitting through a John Wayne action film called "The High and the Mighty" at the Fabulous Fox Theater, a movie palace like I've never seen, with an inside that was closer to Cleopatra's temple than anything else. It also had comfortably cool air, and I treated myself to a popcorn and weiner dinner and sat through the movie two straight times. They roomed me with bench jockey Jim Brideweser for the road trips, and he was off in the Chase Hotel bar with his teammates until about two in the morning when he stumbled in smelling like gin and woke me up so I couldn't get back to sleep. Not a great start to the trip, but at the least the game I was following was a heckuva gas.

7/13: EXIT STAGE NORTH

My new Masters "pals" were edgy after their one-run loss in the series opener, but felt the second game was in their favor with 13-game winner Mike Garcia facing George Zuverink. Even my roomie Jim Brideweser was running his utility mouth at breakfast.

—"Mike punishes right-hand hitters, so if he can stop Frazier and Fox and Slaughter and the Duke, we'll shave their butts."

That didn't sound too promising or appealing, but when their second hitter of the game Gus Bell cracked one off Zuvie into the right field pavilion, I opened my eyes. Too bad Joe Frazier picked this day to not be worthless, as he doubled and scored on a Fox single to tie the game right away. Garcia did take care of Snider (zero-for-5 on the afternoon), but other Flips got to him, especially Eddie Yost with two doubles and Kiner with an RBI double.

Tied 3-3 with Jim McDonald on the bump in the last of the 10th and the Flipside relief legal team of Kinder & Mossi having already replaced Zuverink, Andy Seminick stepped up with two outs and skied one over my head as I kneeled near the Masters dugout and way down the left field line—where it scraped off the foul pole and into the bleachers for a game-winning homer! [on a 1-2 chance] The Flipside players poured from the dugout and pounded Andy into meat loaf when he reached home plate, and I was careful to hide my little smirk.

That smirk vanished the second I entered the Masters' locker room, where Frank Thomas had already turned over the food table and McDonald was soaking himself in the shower with his uniform still on. Many players tended to give me evil glances and stay far away from me when I dressed after a loss, and this time I may as well have had leprosy.

I slipped outside early, intending to take the streetcar back to the hotel instead of the team bus, but for some reason a fancy black car was waiting for me at the curb with its back door open.

—"Get in, Paul," said a familiar voice from the back seat, and I slid in beside Joe DiMaggio.

"What the heck are you doing here?" I asked.

—"Never mind, because we're about to be there."

"Where??"

—"You're flying back to Milwaukee with me for tomorrow's doubleheader. Some busher named Vern Thies threw a three-hit shutout at us today, so I need some good luck company against those red menacing Commies. You seem to have the Masters hexed for now, right?"

He didn't even give me time to answer. The car whisked me off to a small local airport, where Joe's little chartered plane was waiting, the alibi I was gonna tell Brideweser over the phone already forming in my head.

MOS 100 001 010 0 - 3 7 2
FLP 100 000 020 1 - 4 10 1
W-Mossi L-McDonald
HRS: Bell, Seminick
GWRBI-Seminick

7/15: SPOOKY STUFF IN MILWAUKEE

I got back to my room at the Pfister Hotel kind of late after watching the Clockers and Bombs game down in Chicago, and was surprised that Jim Brideweser wasn't there yet. Matter of fact he was on a cot in the same room as Adams and Morgan because he insisted that Room 638 that I was in was one of the haunted ones. Sure enough, the Pfister had a reputation for ghost sightings through the years, and Brideweser apparently had the guts of a three-year-old. He took quite a bunch of ribbing from Adams-Morgan until he told them to shut up or he'd make them suffer.

Funny, but I did have a lousy sleep there my first night because I thought someone in the room above me was dragging something across the floor. This time I ducked down to the hotel bar before it closed for a nightcap, thinking at the least a drink would help me pass out, and on my way back to the elevator through the lobby I looked up and saw this fetching brunette staring at me from an upper balcony. Thing was, she was wearing a dress out of the late 1800s and was as pale as…well, a ghost. And when I raced up a flight of stairs to the balcony, she had weirdly vanished. There was no dragging sound in Room 638 that night, but I gotta admit I was secretly hoping for a woman's mournful sigh.

7/16: DON'T GET THE WHITE HURT ANGRY

I should've known. The Masters took their series finale with the Flips in St. Louis when I wasn't around, and now that I was ball-manning for them in Milwaukee, bad things were happening again. Starting with a strangely lousy outing by Bob Rush and an unexpected, ridiculously good one by Billy Hoeft, who was new to the Red Menace rotation. Billy had a 3-hitter going through six innings and hadn't allowed a hit since the 3rd. The Menace took a 2-1 lead in the 5th on an Avila double, Noren's third straight single and a Mueller sac fly, and then everything fell apart in a Rush in the 7th when Vic Wertz beat out a force grounder, scored moments later on a three-run Finigan homer, and the rout was on.

While the Menace were racking up four more scores in the 8th off the dregs of the Masters pen, Thomas stormed around in the outfield and made sure to bump into me when he came into the dugout.

—"Thanks for everything, mascot turd," he muttered.

"Thought you didn't believe in superstition," I snapped back. I thought his crewcut was going to ignite, but I just walked away and continued to do my job. Thomas took his frustrations out on the baseball instead of my head in the 9th with the game out of reach and hit a Bob Miller pitch that probably landed somewhere in Arkansas.

—"Don't mind Frank," said Brideweser later, still spooked on his cot in Adams and Morgan's room, "He just needs someone or something to hate."

7/17: ANOTHER PARTY AT OZZIE & HARRIET'S

I was up at 6 a.m. yesterday because I smelled strong perfume, right before some creepy presence in Room 638 grabbed the bottom of my blanket and tugged it off my legs. I jumped up, half-awake.

"Marilyn? Grace??"

If only I were that lucky. Actually, Miss Kelly finally joined the team on the road trip after we dropped the first game to the Menace so she could lecture some of the boys on their hitting in her penthouse suite upstairs. The trip would be just five more games—three against the Blackboards in Pittsburgh and two more in the Bronx against the Pinstripe Lagoons after the all-star break, but Grace brought enough suitcases and clothing along for an African safari.

—"Hank is a sweet and gentle giant," she whispered to me from her field box at Marx Field, "But that Thomas fellow needed more spanking when he was young. He won't do a thing unless it's his own idea."

It was sure hard to argue with anything the White Hurt did yesterday. After Red Wilson cracked a solo homer to begin the scoring against Harry Dorish in the 3rd, Sauer singled and Thomas put another ball in orbit, then added two singles and a double to help us build a 5-1 lead.

But the Reds have been Menacing against the Masters all year, and began pummeling Chuck Stobbs with zeal in the 7th, dispatching him to the showers with three singles and a walk to start his inning. Bill Tremel entered, got Finigan on a huge double play ball and Avila on a grounder and the score was 5-3 to the 8th. Then little Chico Carrasquel socked one to start the Menace 8th, and unflappable Jim McDonald came in to predictably retire all six batters he faced and close things out.

We boarded the train to Pittsburgh, where we'd have another day off, and I was already wondering how I'd get into trouble there.

7/19: CHAKALES MAGIC ACT IS NOTHING TO CHUCKLE ABOUT

A day off in Pittsburgh is a little better than a day off in Jersey City, because the local beer is better and there's more pool halls to gamble in, but I even missed out on that fun by getting in late from St. Louis. The team was staying on Mellon Square at the fancy William Penn Hotel, which was almost 40 years old and was where Count Basie once played and Bob Hope proposed to his wife, among other things, It was also where Brideweser agreed to room with me again because I wasn't in a haunted chamber, and as you'll read in a second, the timing couldn't have been better for him.

In a completely weird series opener, Don Liddle faced Bob Chakales at Forbes Jungle Park and it was scoreless somehow for the first three innings, the Blackboards and us leaving a combined eleven people on base. The Boards then scored twice in the 4th on a Jablonski single, Dave Philley double, and two-run single by Chucklin' Chakales! No one was laughing in our dugout, because it didn't take long before we realized we were facing a modern Harry Houdini. I may have been collecting baseballs in rapid time on the field and ignoring insults slinging my way from pimple-faced Delby the Blackboards batboy, but the Masters left the bases packed four times in the game and kept losing infielders. First Gil McDougald got plunked and knocked out for a dozen games, and then Bobby Morgan fouled out and twisted something, and my roomie Brideweser was called in to "play" shortstop, hitting into the team's only DP his first time up and throwing one in the stands to lead to a third Blackboards run in the 7th! Sauer went hitless again with an 0-for-5 day and we left 13 on the bases total, Jolly coming in to whiff Sauer and end the game after Chuckles loaded the sacks with his sixth, seventh, and eighth walks in the 9th. Grace Kelly finally showed up at the hotel with her entourage after dinner, but was all pissy and wasn't talking to reporters or anybody on the team. Wouldn't want to be her butler in the morning.

7/20: AMAZING GRACE, CONTINUED

Frank Thomas snatched the front of my uniform as I trudged back up the tunnel after his team dropped another game at Forbes Jungle Park, all ready to put the white hurt on me.

—"Two in a row to these bums? What's your game, punk?"

"Well, the Blackboards ain't bums. They're tied for first in the other division, and since they got Pee Wee—"

—"Shut your hole. Compared to us they're bums. Garcia just don't give up seven runs in an inning. What've you been doing to his balls?"

"I haven't touched his balls. You see me out there, Frank. I barely have time to collect them and and feed the umpire, let alone—"

"You better pray your mascot ball ass is clean." He shoved me aside and marched to the clubhouse to no doubt wreak more havoc. And I got the hell away from the the park quick as I could, holed up in my hotel room and waited till midnight to hit the William Penn downstairs bar, perfectly called the Speakeasy.

I smelled the French perfume after only two scotches. Looked to my right and there was Grace Kelly seated at the bar a few feet away, half-hidden with a light blue shawl over her head. Drinking what looked like a pink Cosmopolitan. She winked at me and motioned for me to slide over.

—"Rumor has it that Mr. Thomas is treating you unfairly."

"You could say that."

—"Mmmm. I just did. Do you have a cigarette, Paulie? I'm plum out of them."

I told her I didn't smoke, but the bartender obliged in no time and even lit it for her.

—"Should I be worried, Paulie? We haven't exactly been a powerhouse of late, and nights like tonight I fear for my continued employment."

"Naw, you're great. I mean—you're doing great, Miss Kelly."

—"Grace. Remember?" She clinked her pink glass against mine, then sighed. "Being an actress is awfully hard work, but people don't realize how tough a job it is to instruct fellows' hitting on the road on these lonnng, lonnng trips with little else to do...Understand?"

"Sure. Will you be going to Philadelphia for the All-Star Game?"

—"Oh of course! It's where I'm from, you know."

"I didn't know that."

—"Mmmm. Well now you do." She finished off her drink in one large sip and stared at me. "How do you do that thing with your hair, anyway?"

"W-what thing?"

She reached out and ran a slender finger through a black curl on my forehead.

–"This. It's rather cute."

The ice in my glass dissolved on the spot from my suddenly warm hand. The bartender re-appeared.

–"You folks want another round?"

–"I think not," said Grace. "This gentlemen is going to help me find my room." She woozily got off her stool. "My, I think I've even forgotten the number!" Took my arm and walked me to the lounge door. Then leaned into my ear inside her perfume cloud and whispered, "919…"

7/21: A BRAND NEW FLIPPIN' WORLD

It's okay to hate me now. Every player on the Masters suddenly did, even the slumping, formerly gentle giant Hank Sauer, who instead of offering me a pre-game tobacco chew like he normally did, spit his out and walked away from me at the batting cage without making eye contact. Heck, even the home plate ump snickered and called me Frenchy during the game when I brought him balls, and this was after Delby the Blackboards cretin batboy, started in on me.

—"Hey dork!" He pointed at the still-red hickey on my neck. "How was Dracula's daughter last night?"

"Wouldn't you like to know?"

—"Is he a no-good Commie spy too?"

"Shut your face."

I was actually expecting this, and knew it came with the dreamy memory of our hitting coach's soft hands and the vodka and perfume scents she combined so well. Bianca Ballorino and Marge Koshinsky were distant memories now, and my biggest challenge with Grace was going to be keeping my name out of the newspaper. She sat in her field box at Forbes Jungle Park with dark glasses for the last game and smiled in my direction whenever I glanced at her, and twice I nearly had whistling drives crack off my noggin.

Knowledge of my midnight rendezvous seemed to bond her hitters, though, as Sauer, who believe it or else is 8-for-his-last-70 (.114) with one home run in July, singled in the 1st to help them score twice against Leo Kiely. Then after the Boards tied it in the 4th on triples by Temple and the returned Minoso and a single by Borkowski, four singles in the 5th put them ahead for good before McDonald polished off the final four outs for Bob Rush.

"What was it really like, roomie?" asked Brideweser at the station after the game, continuing the theme.

"Better than a cold one in a hammock," I said, and started to enter the train, but a guy in a chauffeur uniform steered me away, and over to a fancy town car waiting at a nearby curb. With Grace in the backseat.

"Ride with me to Philadelphia for the All-Star Game, Paulie," she cooed, already dressed in the third outfit I'd seen her in that day, "We'll stay with my parents, who I'm sure will be delighted to meet you!"

7/23: HENRIETTA'S QUAIL AND THE HALF-STAR GAME

The lordly Kelly House was in a section of Philly I didn't know existed called East Falls, and was bigger than our entire apartment building in Brooklyn. A colored butler opened the door for us and Grace's tall and fit dad John came out to greet us wearing a tie under a navy sweater, along with her pretty mom Margaret.

—"And what line of work are you in again, Paulie?" asked Mr. Kelly in no time in the drawing room over gin and tonics. "Our daughter has told us nothing about you."

"During the game I gather the team's—Actually it's called Baseball Equipment Management."

—"And what neighborhood do you live in up in New York City?" asked his wife.

"Prospect Park," I answered, which was a bit of a lie, but at that point I was just trying to keep my head above water.

We "repaired" to the block-long dining room for a dinner of Maryland Quail in Plum Sauce, scalloped potatoes flown in from Idaho, and Waldorf Salad. The quails were dainty and hard to cut with a knife and I was just sitting there dying for a big old turkey leg I could eat with my hand. Grace had insisted I wear the nice sport jacket and tie she bought for me, but she was so far across the table and behind a candleholder it was hard to even see her.

—"Are you not enjoying Henrietta's Quail, Mr. Rubin?" asked Grace's mother.

"Who?"

—"Henrietta. Our cook!"

"Oh, no. It's delicious. I'm just a little full from some road food we had near Harrisburg, so…"

Mrs. Kelly frowned, returned to her plate.

—"Tell me who's going to win the big all-star game tomorrow, Paulie," said Mr. Kelly, "Being in equipment management you must hear some good rumors I can use to my advantage with an Atlantic City wager."

At least that was a subject I could relate to, and went on for a few minutes about the strong Ricky & Lucy Division hitters and the tough Ozzie & Harriet Division pitchers until it was Grace who interrupted me.

—"Paulie knows as well as anyone that the Ozzies don't have a fruit fly's chance against our swaggering Rickys. I can't imagine it will even be close."

We slept in separate bedrooms that were about a half mile away, and I dreamed I was being roasted on a spit in the Kellys' huge back yard. Man, I couldn't wait to get to Shibe Park.

OZZIE & HARRIETS 10, RICKY & LUCY 5

Well, so much for Grace Kelly's baseball expertise. Tom Poholsky threw a scoreless first three innings while Bob Lemon got hammered by Irv Noren (solo homer), Snider, Avila, and Reese (two doubles and a single) in his two-frame outing, and the Ozzies rolled from there. Pee Wee added a two-run homer off Billy Pierce and a sac fly to cap an idiotic four-run 7th that saw them score four times on six walks and no hits. Nearly all of the all-stars got into the game, and the Rickys made it somewhat competitive with two runs in the 8th and three in the 9th on a pinch three-run homer by Gil McDougald off Wilhelm before Mossi got Moon on a weak ground ball to end it.

Grace and I sat in a private box above the Shibe Park rabble, and the game was so dull for her she spent it making telephone calls to her movie friends in Los Angeles. Later in East Falls again, I told her parents my room was a bit stuffy and chose to sleep in one of the spare servant's bedrooms, where I shared a re-laxing beer with Old Tom, Henrietta's butler husband. The next night I'd be back in my Brooklyn bed, and couldn't wait.

R&L 000 000 023 - 5 9 2
O&H 121 200 40x - 10 9 1
W-Poholsky L-Lemon
HRS: Noren, Reese, McDougald
GWRBI-Noren
GAME MVP: Pee Wee Reese

7/25. FLIPSIDES CLOCK THE ROCKERS WITH THEIR A AND B SIDES IN MOTOWN

Yep, it was nice to get a nice relaxing sleep in Brooklyn, but I forgot that Pop would be all riled up in the morning.

—"Two against your Master Boys in the Bronx starting today and the Lagoons are gonna smoke 'em twice!"

"Sure Pop. Have you looked at the standings?"

—"Once an hour, but who cares? Nothing more dangerous than a pack of starving hyenas with nothing to lose!"

Actually, his pinstriped swamp hyenas had dropped eight of eleven to the Masters in all sorts of icky ways, but that didn't sway him, and it didn't for the 46,000 or so other Lagoonites who packed the place for the matinee. To honor the occasion, Pop had invited along his pal Bert Gortnik and squirreled down to some choice box seats behind the Lagoon dugout where they sat with their cigars and made a general rooting racket. I was busy kneeling behind the visiting on-deck circle and glancing up at Grace Kelly, leaning out of a box on the club level in dark glasses while various male fans whistled at her.

Meanwhile, the Masters' offense sputtered some more against disappointing Whitey Ford, who walked four guys and hit another but was never in any trouble after the 1st. Herm Wehmeier was throwing good, too, and it was a tight 1-1 duel through the middle innings. Pop called me over to the seats after I chased down a runaway ball near the home dugout. He and Bert had already drank one too many Ballantines.

—"Paulie! Tell Bert about your buddy DiMaggio!"

"Quiet, Pop!" I whispered. The last thing I wanted was some of the Lagoon players hearing about my "side job" and having it get back to the Masters.

—"Yeah yeah yeah. Rub some bad luck on Wehmeier's balls for us, would ya? We're gettin' tired over here."

Herm got fresh ones from the home plate ump for the last of the 8th, but it didn't matter Busby got himself plunked with the first pitch and then red-hot Musial put the next one into the upper deck to explode the joint!

—"STAN'S MY MAN MUSIAL!!" screamed Pop over and over and the Lagoons had a 3-1 lead. Ford served up a Ray Katt dinger with two outs in the 9th, then whiffed Bobby Morgan and jiminy creepin crickets, the Bikini Bombs were suddenly just four games back in the loss column and I was a leper in the Masters clubhouse for no reason again. I couldn't even look at Grace Kelly afterwards, which may have been the first time any man could ever say that.

MOS 100 000 001 - 2 4 1
BLM 100 000 02x - 3 7 1
W-Ford L-Wehmeier
HRS: Katt, Musial
GWRBI-Musial

7/26: WHOLE LOTTA STREAKIN' GOIN' ON

—"Better scat, Paulie," said Brideweser in the clubhouse right after the Masters got suffocated in their beds by Johnny Antonelli. "Frank Thomas is looking for you."

I figured as much. Since I took their ball-man job on July 5th, the Masters were a dead even 8-8, but suddenly no one on the team could hit, and the White Hurt was erupting because after he provided one of only two of their hits leading off the 2nd, he was gunned down trying to score on a Katt fly ball when Jim Busby smoked him at the plate on a 65% safe chance to end the inning.

"Hey man," I told Brideweser while I laced up my sneakers, "Ain't my fault Musial is hotter than a chili pot right now." Stan's latest game-deciding homer came in the 1st off the inexplicably employed Chuck Stobbs, who was booted off the mound after his single-walk-single-walk-single sequence began the Lagoons' 4th. Clem Labine entered and fired four shutout innings, but the game was long over thanks to Antonelli, who had no problem with the all-righthanded Masters lineup.

I went searching for Grace afterwards and amazingly found her enjoying a Cosmo in her club level box.

—"Oh don't worry about that brute, Paulie. I'll give Frank a nice verbal spanking in the morning and I'm sure he'll enjoy it. We'll be fine as soon as we get home against the Coonskin Caps tomorrow."

"You sure? We weren't too fine against the Black Lagoons!"

—"Mmm. Baseball is a long season, sweetheart." She ran a hand through my hair. "Calm...and patience...and thoughtfulness...can take you a long way..."

"Okay, but—"

—"Have you ever been to Oyster Bay?"

I couldn't tell her that I was dumped on her house's lawn in the middle of the night about a month ago, so I said no, and the next thing I knew her driver was whisking us out to her palace

on the water. The place was stunning and the ocean view hypnotic, as was my host. Aside from Grace, though, the only thing
that kept me from envisioning Frank Thomas' enraged face all
night was the sight of my pop dancing his way out of the Pinstripe Lagoon grandstand after the game with an empty popcorn
box on his head.

First thing this morning, I called our apartment and Pop answered.

—Hey Paulie, heckuva whitewash last night!"

"Sure was."

—"And it's a good thing you called."

"Why's that?"

—"Because Joe DiMaggio's looking for you."

7/27: NOWHERE TO HIDE, EXCEPT OYSTER BAY

Pop got it wrong. Joe actually came back from Cleveland early
because watching his team lose games to the K2s was making
him sick. Anyway, without telling him I was canoodling with
Grace Kelly, I said I'd meet him in his private booth at the Carn-
egie Deli for a late breakfast. Of course that meant telling Grace
my stomach wasn't up for a morning sail in the bay.

—"Such a busy, busy boy!" she said.

"Didn't you call me a ball man recently?"

—"Mmmm. Whatever you are, Paulie, see you at Rear Window Stadium for the matinee, when I promise we'll make those
Coonskins cry."

By contrast, Joe was a little beaten down and looked like he'd
had five cups of coffee already.

—"Great job with whatever you've been doing to the Masters'
offense, Paul."

"Actually I haven't done a thing. Their bats were hot as beje-
ezus the first three months and now they can't hit a kids balloon."

—"Yeah, well now I'm worried about MY team because when
we're not getting hurt we're stinking up the place. Did you know

we're 13 games out of first now?"

"Right. Though it's still only July—

—"On top of that I haven't been able to reach Marilyn on the phone for three days. Her agent and manager are lying right in my ear, I know it."

"Sorry to hear about that..."

—"So do me a favor and come out to our doubleheader today with the Bikini Bombs. Maybe you just being in the stands will help."

"Uhhhhh—"

—"Great. I'll leave a pass at the third base gate."

I called Grace around noon, lied to her that I was under the weather and maybe I'd catch her that night. Little did I know that Oyster Bay would become my fallout shelter.

7/28: ALL THINGS COME TO AN END—EVENTUALLY

Thankfully the 2-1 game in Baltimore was only 90 minutes long, because I was able to get back to Oyster Bay by midnight and sit on one of its outside decks with Grace and watch the moonlight on the water for an hour. When I asked her how the mood was at Rear Window Stadium that day after her team's latest disaster, she just shushed me.

—"Things just happen sometimes, dear heart. Your life can be as charmed as you can ever imagine and suddenly—whoosh, there goes the rug from under your feet. So I wouldn't be concerned with those Master boys. I'm going to push for a new lineup order tomorrow which should be enough to distract them and perhaps even fetch them their next win."

"Okay, but Thomas is still going to turn me into mincemeat—"

—"Fiddlesticks. He's all bluster." She squeezed closer to me and took my hand. "I'm falling for you, Paulie. You're tough and I feel safe around you and you're fun to be with and so different from some of the conceited scoundrels I've been with. Promise me you'll stick with me through this difficult stretch, darling."

I promised her. And we began to kiss…

* * *

The next morning I stopped at the newsstand before I dared to go to the stadium again, just to check in with Pop. He wasn't there yet but Schnozzo was, setting things up.

—"Sheesh, never thought I'd see you again. Good timing. Some dame called for you a little while ago and left this phone number."

It sure wasn't Grace's number. I went to the back of the stand, dialed it, and a breathless, very distraught Marilyn Monroe picked up the phone.

—"Oh, Paulie, something awful happened last night! Remember Hal Schaefer?"

"Uhh, who?"

—"My voice coach! I've been…you know…dating him a bit behind Joe's back, and yesterday they found him unconscious in his bungalow at Fox and he's in the hospital now and might die and oh God I need to get out of town and can I fly there and be with you again for a few days?"

"W-what about Joe?"

—"I don't know! Maybe I'll see him and apologize and maybe I won't! But you've been such a good escort for me while I'm there and you calm me down and my plane arrives tomorrow morning, okay??"

"Well…"

—"Thank you, sweetie. THANK YOU!" And she hung up.

7/29: NATIONAL HEART ATTACK DAY

Before I rented another car and drove to LaGuardia Airport, I decided to take no chances this time and stopped at a costume store. The phony moustache and glasses and curly wig worked just fine, though it took a good ten seconds for Marilyn to recognize me when she came off the plane wearing her same grey wig, black dress and veil. At least it made her giggle for one second, because when she lifted her veil in the car it looked like she hadn't slept in three days.

—"It's so awful, Paulie, Hal's stomach was full of sleeping pills and Benzedrine and was washed down with typewriter cleaning fluid, and I don't know if he'll make it—" She broke down in tears.

"What about Joe? Does he know about…you and him?"

—"No, but I'm sure he suspects. He has friends everywhere, y'know?"

"Yeah, I know."

—"How do you know?"

"Because I'm always…reading about him. Let's get you a room and find you some food, okay?"

—"Okay…But why did you wear a disguise?"

"Well, in case some nosy photographer recognizes you. No use gettin' MY photo in the paper, right? Joe's team is back in town and so is he, and like you say, he has people everywhere."

—"Oh, I don't give a damn anymore. I like New York as much as he does because there are great acting teachers here who say they'll work with me and my friend Arthur Miller the playwright is here, and I don't want to be afraid of Joe anymore or leashed to him like a dog—"

"And how about we get you a nice cup of hot tea."

There was no chance in hell I'd be calling Joe to see what he wanted, or going anywhere near Oyster Bay or Rear Window Stadium. With Marilyn finally asleep up in her room, I hung around the Picadilly Hotel lobby most of the day and followed the ball games on one of the bellboy's portable radios. Believe you me, there was a lot to follow.

7/30: NORMA JEAN, BAR THE DOORS

On my way to a nearby deli to fetch Marilyn a corned beef sandwich, I stopped at a phone booth to finally get back to Joe, who had been trying me at home again.

—"Where you been, kid? We're thirteen behind in the loss column and lucky to win that one yesterday against the Bombs with Mantle and Furillo out."

"I know, but I thought you were paying me to mess with the Masters."

—"Yeah, and you have been, but even they squeaked out a win yesterday, so what gives with that? Anyway, you hear about this Hollywood *stronzo* Hal Schaefer who went off in an ambulance to get his stomach pumped?"

"Uhh, I think I did. Who was that again?"

—"A voice coach jerk Marilyn was hiding the cannoli with, I suspect. Another week of that and I would've been the one sending him to the hospital. No wonder I wasn't able to get ahold of her."

"Geez. Gotta be tough married to someone that famous…"

—"Tough being married to anyone, kid. You'll find out."

I quickly hung up and called Grace, who told me I was "welcome" back at Rear Window Stadium anytime now that the Masters had pulled out another win, and would I please join her in the box for the first big game with the Bikini Bombs that night? I said I had a few "important errands" but would try and make it.

Except when I got back to the Picadilly with Marilyn's sandwich, Marilyn wasn't in the room. I paced around in a panic, checked the hallway and stairwell and fire escape, then saw her come out of the elevator toting a little white pharmacy bag. She didn't look good.

—"Sorry, Paulie. I just had to pick up a few more sleeping pills at the corner."

Then I saw that she wasn't wearing her grey old lady wig or even her dark glasses. I quickly got her back in her room and took the elevator to the lobby.

Oh crap. At least two dozen reporters and photographers were pouring into the hotel from the street!

Marilyn had already downed a couple of the pills, so I had to practically carry her down the one stairwell on the floor that didn't trigger an alarm. Got her out to an alley and propped her up in a doorway while I ran for my car. The front of the hotel was a newspaperman mob scene.

"Quick! Where does your friend Arthur Miller live?"

—"Some big building…Central Park…" She was falling against my shoulder in the front seat.

"Which one??"

—"Can't remember…I'll know it when I see it."

Nobody was following us, but with the midday traffic it still took half an hour to get to the road around the park so I could shake Marilyn awake and help her recognize which building it was.

—"Arthur's a nice man…You'll like him, Paulie."

"Great. I'll meet him some other time. Which building is it??"

—"Oh…That one."

I pounded the brake, double parked, hauled her out, then kept her on her feet at the front door while I rang Miller's apartment buzzer. A desk man for the building came out and stood there in mild shock.

"This is Marilyn Monroe. Get her up to Arthur Miller's place and be quiet about it." I handed him a ten-dollar bill and the half-asleep famous actress and took off with visions of Bombs vs. Masters pennant race baseball in my head.

Marilyn was certainly a nice person, but it seemed to me she lived her life like a candle in a breeze sometimes.

7/31: ALL KINDS OF SCRIPT-FLIPPING IN PLAY TODAY

We interrupt your regularly scheduled Paulie shenanigans to take you straight to the pennant race showdown dramas in Pittsburgh and Brooklyn…

BLACKBOARDS 7, FLIPSIDES 6

Oh lawdy, what a game in Pittsburgh. With a pitching matchup for the ages in Bob Feller (12-3) vs. Tom Poholsky (16-2), everything comes up roses for the Flips early as they pummel Poho for nine hits and five runs, Snider driving in two with a single and sac fly. It's 6-0 when Pee Wee Reese knocks a solo homer in the last of the 6th, and then luck begins to change...or flip. Two walks and a single load the sacks in the last of the 7th, and when Slaughter drops a pinch fly ball by Dale Mitchell for a two-base error, it's 6-3. Feller bails himself out of that mess and sets the Boards down 1-2-3 in the 8th, but his shaky 7th has Flipside management worried, and saves leader Don Mossi enters for the 9th.

Things quickly get uglier than him. Pitcher Bob Chakales pinch hits with a leadoff double. Nieman pinch hits too and flies out, but Piersall rips a single to make it 6-4. Ray Jablonski bats for Marlowe and bounces a game-ending DP ball to Alvin Dark. I don't have to tell you that Alvin throws the ball halfway to Scranton, but yeah, he does, and runners are at second and third. Reese walks, and Ellis Kinder is quickly hailed to face Temple. Who walks to make it 6-5. Up steps Frankie Baumholtz, dangerous pepper-pot, who lines a single into center to score the tying and winning runs and put Forbes Jungle Park up for grabs! Back into first go the Blackboard Seven, who will send Chakales to the hill against George Zuverink after they travel to St. Louis for the next two games.

FLP 101 301 000 - 6 10 2
BBS 000 001 204 - 7 8 1
W-Marlowe L-Mossi
HR: Reese
GWRBI-Baumholtz

MASTERS 3, BOMBS 2

I'm back in my ball-man uniform for this one, as ex-Tribers Early Wynn and Mike Garcia stage a fine duel. A Jensen single and Schoendienst double plate a Bikini run in the 1st, and with the Masters bats unproductive again, stranding ten runners in the first six innings, it becomes 2-0 Bombs in the 7th on a Miranda single, sac bunt, and RBI hit by Jensen.

Gus Bell, with a walk and two singles from the third spot in the order, rubs his bat on me again near the on-deck circle and works a one-out walk. Frank Thomas then clubs Wynn's first pitch high and deep and gone to tie the game! With Jim McDonald resting, Chet Nichols takes over when Garcia tires and allows nothing in an inning and a third, before Bill Tremel escapes two baserunners in the 9th. Adams and Bell make outs in the last of the 9th, and here comes cleanup man Thomas again. He swings and puts a white hurt on that ball like I've never seen for an even longer game-winning homer and a sweep of the two-game set with the Bombs! In the clubhouse, Frank gives in under pressure from his shouting teammates and rubs his bat over every inch of my uniform until I get a rash. At least the Johnnie Walkers and giant porterhouse steak he buys me later stops me from itching it.

BKB 100 000 100 - 2 12 1
MOS 000 000 201 - 3 8 0
W-Tremel L-Wynn
HRS: Thomas-2
GWRBI-Thomas

8/1: MEET MY NEW PAL, THE WHITE HURT

So Frank Thomas was my new bench buddy when the Masters were in the dugout. Hank Sauer has gone from real hot to real cold this season, but the White Hurt has stayed dangerously warm, and after avoiding me like the plague after I "joined" the club back on July 4th, he was suddenly filling my ear with personal histories whether I wanted to hear them or not.

—"My dad was a one-armed hospital laundry worker in Pittsburgh, and I can't believe he wanted me to be a priest. Bet you didn't know I entered a seminary in Niagara Falls when I was a teenager!"

"You're right. I mean I didn't—"

"And you'd think Branch Rickey would've given me a raise on the Pirates after '53. But El Cheapo wouldn't budge. They put the left field fence back to 365 feet after they traded Ralph Kiner to the Cubs, and my homer-hitting suffered. They could've just re-named Kiner's Korner 'Frank's Fence' or something!"

Frank had an awful day at the plate, 0-for-4 with a pair of double plays, probably because he was too busy blabbing at me every half inning. But it didn't mean a mosquito, because the Masters were back getting their famous luck in force, with Sauer hitting two singles and only his second homer in a month, with Bobby Adams getting on base four out of five times, and with Jackie Robinson already conveniently hurt for the K2s, their hottest stick Sam Mele going out for the rest of the series after his second at bat. Rush got knocked out in the 8th, but with first and third, no one out and the score shaved to 6-4, the unlikely duo of Chet Nichols and Bill Tremel retired the last seven K2s of the game, keeping the Suspenser lead at four and a half.

8/2: WHITEY AND TOBY AND GET OUTTA TOWN

Now Arthur Miller was calling me at home. Marilyn was driving him daffy after just one day at his apartment, and he had a play he was trying to finish. So after stopping at the newsstand to help Pop and Schnozzo set up, I threw my cheap disguise back on, scooped up Marilyn from the building on Central Park without one photographer seeing us, and bee-lined her to La Guardia for a necessary flight home.

—"Turns out my friend may be in the hospital for a real long time, Paulie," she breathed, "so I guess I should be with him if I can."

"The heck with Hal. What about Joe? He has no idea you were even here and his team is in the trash can right now!"

—"I don't care. Joe hasn't been nice to me. He just hates the business I'm in and anybody connected to it, and he has no right to tell me who to be friends with." She gave me a saucy cheek-kiss. "You're always nice, Paulie. Maybe you can come see me in L.A. some time!"

"Please don't start."

I walked her to her airport gate without any fuss, then skedaddled back to Brooklyn and Rear Window Stadium for our night game with the K2s—and wished I hadn't.

Lefty Dean Stone was bewildering every Masters hitter, throwing a no-hitter into the 7th, when my best buddy Frank Thomas broke it up with a one-out single. But the K2s had already scored four times off Stobbs replacement Clem Labine with a flurry of singles and doubles. Bobby Hofman then cut the lead in half with a two-run poke, and that's how the game ended.

We were so punchless I began following the end of Joe's game with the Caps across town—which was beyond belief. When he phoned me in the quiet clubhouse afterwards, I was expecting him to be all enthralled and telling me about it. Instead I could feel his disturbed mood through the phone wire.

"—I just found out Marilyn was in town, and didn't call me. And that some local degenerate was escorting her around. Why don't we meet at Toots Shor's later tonight and discuss how we can find this guy."

"Uhhhh…yeah okay probably maybe."

Our express up to Boston for our series with the Coonskins was leaving in ninety minutes. Even with every Masters player except Thomas not thrilled to have me around that day, there was no way in Hades I wasn't getting on that friggin' train.

8/3: ON VACATION WITH POKER AND CLAMS

Grace wasn't making the Boston trip, having to "meet with Hitch" in London for three days to discuss her next picture with him. "See you in the Windy City for the Bombs series, perhaps?" she purred. That was sure fine with me. With no needy celebrity dames or an angry Clipper to worry about, my train ride up to

Beantown with the team was a royal gas, more than three hours of poker games, fat cigars, and beer bottles. Gus Bell beat my straight flush with a royal one, but I won everything back with a surprise full house on Cunningham that got him cursing me with every drop of Irish slang he knew. They put us up at the Copley Plaza, and Final Frontier Field was stuffed with Caps fans the next afternoon, even though they'd dealt away a lot of good players to our rival Bombs.

Too bad for them. Even after Jim Gilliam popped Don Liddle's first pitch into the left field net in the last of the 1st, we weren't worried, because the usually disappointing Virgil Trucks was going for them. He broke his axle right away in the 2nd, when with one out, Cunningham doubled, Hoak singled, Liddle doubled, Morgan walked, Bell doubled, Wilson singled, Thomas doubled, and we had five runs in a flash. Sauer, dropped into the sixth spot again, went zero-for-five but it didn't even matter, because Liddle shut the Coonskins down the rest of the way for the easy win, and it was clams with bellies at the Union Oyster House later. I realize I'm supposed to be putting the whammy on these Masters somehow, but Joe is kind of a jerk, Grace is a living doll, and to be honest, hanging around with winners is a lot more fun. As long as it lasts…

8/4: THE COLOSSUS OF DUSTY RHODES

This time it was Pop calling me at the hotel, waking me up from another clam and beer hangover.

—"We beat the DiMaggios twice, Paulie! And Dusty got the big blow both times! Me and Bert were there for the whole thing!"

"That's nice, Pop. So the Lagoons are like twenty games out now?"

—"Yeah, but just four behind the DiMaggios! Can you imagine if we can finish fourth?"

(One thing about Pop, he was the King of the Silver Lining.)

"More important, has anyone I know been calling our place, like Joe?"

—"Not on my watch. Your mother's visiting her cousins in Teaneck. How long are you on the road for?"

"Three here, and three with the Bombs in Chicago, so Thursday night."

—"Okay. Better let them Bombs beat ya!"

"Sure, Pop."

The way things were going for us in Boston, I wouldn't put money on that. Garcia vs. Loes sure was a mismatch, though the Caps were tougher this time, and trailed 4-2 in the 9th when McDonald started getting wild. But in his first game back, Gil McDougald turned a nifty 4-6-3 double play on Gilliam after walks to Shantz and Aaron, and we had our 66th win. The bigger news was that Sauer was back in the cleanup spot and notched his 14th game-winner with a sac fly in the 1st, then homered and singled later! Guess that short Coonskin Monster in left was too hard for him to resist.

8/5: MR. COFFEE IS SHORT A FEW POTS

Brideweser shook me awake this morning.

—"Hey. Some wise guy who says he's Joe DiMaggio wants you on the phone."

"Crap. Tell him I'm in the shower."

—"YOU tell him." And he dropped the receiver on my neck. I groaned and dragged the entire phone into the bathroom for some privacy while my roomie went back to sleep.

Joe had either spiked his coffee with something or drank a few. First thing I did was apologize for not meeting him at Toots' the other night, because the team train was leaving earlier than I thought.

—"Forget that for now. I'll find the creep who was showing Marilyn around sooner or later. I just need someone to talk to, kid. Between my rotten marriage and my stinkin' club that just lost three out of four to the Black Lagoons, I'm a big dago mess."

So for the next twenty minutes I buttered him up with questions about his hitting streak in '41, and his MVP seasons, and the Yankee championships he was part of, and that he did the best he could building the DiMaggios this year but sometimes "junk happens."

He had the Summiteers coming in for some games next and I told him to "just get into their bullpen and you'll have a gravy train." And then I said I needed to get back to sleep and hung up.

It's hard to raise ex-heroes…

8/7: JERRY-MANDERED AT THE WRONG TIME

Grace and me both agreed we didn't want anybody to blame another team loss on her being all distracted by our hanky-panky, so last night I roomed with Brideweser again—who was out cold at 10 p.m.—and today I was the first one on the field at Castle Bravo helping get the game's baseballs in order. The home plate ump was a guy named Dusty Boggess, a Scotch-Irish fella from Texas, so if anything I thought he'd give Gil McDougald a break at the plate. Instead, he was just a flat-out jerkface to me.

—"It's 94 out here, cowpoke, and I got a dinner date tonight. How 'bout you hurry it up with them balls?"

It was hot and also muggy on the north side of Chicago, and I was retrieving and collecting and delivering those suckers as fast as I could without passing out. Didn't seem to inspire our hitters, though, and Grace just sat in the shade upstairs and fanned herself with a program all afternoon.

Boggess called five strikeouts against us but also five walks, so he was fair enough. But after getting just five hits off Gromek the day before, this time we only found four against Ruben Gomez, Howie Fox and Steve Ridzik. One of those knocks was a solo homer by Bobby Adams, though, to give Clem Labine a 2-1 lead going to the 7th. Then that annoying Jackie Jensen popped a solo shot to tie it up, and against McDonald an inning later, ev-

erything melted. Morgan flubbed a Cavaretta grounder for starters, two ground outs got Phil to third, and up stepped pinch-
hitter Jerry Snyder for Miranda, with his 3-for-34 (.088) batting
average, Whack! Single into left for the lead, Ridzik got the last
four guys, and the Bombs had beaten us a second straight day.

—"Those Big Fly Lords are struggling, Paulie," pouted Grace
afterwards, "And we get them at home next, but we simply have
to do better in our finale here. How about I schedule an extra
batting session for the boys tomorrow morning and you help me
with it?"

"Oh, that should go just swell," I lied.

8/8: BOMBING OUT IN BIKINI TOWN

Our "extra batting practice session" in the morning went about
as badly as I thought it might. Grace wore one of her African safari outfits with a pith helmet and spent most of her time giving
Sauer handle grip attention, while I threw low-speed fastballs to
everyone else with most of the players trying to hit line drives at
my legs. Predictably, after two losses in a row, Frank Thomas was
not my friend anymore and took aim at my crotch instead.

But they needed the practice big time, because nine hits in two
tries against these guys wasn't enough. This time they managed
eight—but stretched them over 13 innings. The game turned
out to be a real corker though, with three of them hits, a Wilson homer and triples by Sauer and Thomas, happening on 20%
success chances. Still, Mike Garcia pitched worse than his old
amigo Early Wynn, and we trailed 4-2 into the 9th after bleacher bombs from Jensen and Mays. Sauer's three-bagger then came
after a Wilson walk, and Cunningham tied the game with a
single to send it to extras.

Like, many extras, with many scoring chances. Ray Katt finally
blasted one in the 13th off Jackie Collum for a 5-4 lead, but
bullpen ace McDonald couldn't hold the fort. A Jensen walk and
Schoendienst double allowed Mays to tie it again with a sac fly,

before Phil Cavaretta, already with two walks and three singles in six at bats, stayed in against lefty Nichols and ripped a game-winning double!

While Grace had nothing to say later and took her private jet back to New York, I hunkered down in my seat for the entire train ride. There were no card games, no cigars smoked. No one was mad at me because the players knew how fortunate they were to even get the game to extra innings. All I knew was that I did not envy the Lord of the Big Flies when they took the field in Brooklyn tomorrow.

8/9 : WINNING EASY AND UGLY

It felt weird to sleep in my bed at home last night, but it was also pretty necessary seeing that Pop was up till almost midnight listening to a 15-inning Lagoons game with the Flipsides on the radio, and drank way too many Ballantines to get himself through it. The Masters had a far easier time of it earlier in the evening, which I'll get to soon, but it was a day filled with high and low drama on the '54 ball fields, something I've learned to get used to awful quick. Dig these…

BLACKBOARDS 8, BOMBS 6 (13 innings)

For a second straight day, the Bikinis are put through the washer in Chicago and come out the losing end against the visiting Boards, who lose Pee Wee Reese for the rest of the series in his second at bat but somehow still pull the thing out. Down 2-0 to Billy Pierce, they tie it on a Chakales two-run single, then take a 4-2 lead on the first of two Ray Jablonski bleacher shots. It's 6-4 Boards in the 8th when Berra rips a second triple and Steve Bilko greets Don Johnson with a pinch two-run homer to tie it at six. Eleven pitchers are used in total as the game slogs to the 13th, when two singles and a dropped fly in left by Skinner lead to the two unearned runs that decide the game. Dave Jolly, who has been throwing great after a wild and not-very-jolly first

few months, goes five one-hit innings for the win.
BBS 000 022 110 000 2 - 8 10 0
BKB 100 100 220 000 0 - 6 10 2
W-Jolly L-Hughes
HRS: Jablonski-2, Boone
INJURY: Reese-3

FLIPSIDES 4, LAGOONS 3 (15 innings)

But the Boards & Bombs got nothin' on the Flips & 'Goons.
The Swampers whack three solo homers off Sonny Dixon, but
thanks to a two-run Seminick shot and a Snider RBI single in
the 8th, the teams go into extras tied at three, when a pair of Star
of the Day runner-ups emerge for the Flyin' Flips: Nellie Fox,
who after skying out in his first two at bats, singles his next four
times up, then doubles in Frazier with the winning run in the
15th off Tom Hurd, and Don Mossi, who throws NINE innings
of shutout relief to neutralize Dusty Rhodes and get the win.
Handsome Don will be unable to pitch for many days now, but
they'll apparently worry about that when they have to.
FLP 020 000 010 000 001 - 4 10 0
BLM 100 110 000 000 000 - 3 11 1
W-Mossi L-Turd
HRS: Seminick, Hatton-2, Banks
GWRBI-Fox

DiMAGGIOS 7, DERBIES 4 (10 innings)

The Sunday Dicecast runner-up was this thriller at the Coffee Grounds, where the real Star of the Day shockingly shone.
Trailing 3-2 to Robin Roberts in the 7th, Carl Furillo ties the
game with a solo shot, then after two and two-thirds of shaky
relief from Howie Judson, a Baker double and singles by Gordon
and Kuenn give the Chromers the lead in the 10th. No big deal.
Roberts tires himself out by allowing singles to Goodman and
Collins and walking Rosen for the fourth time to load the bases.
Bob Greenwood comes in and retires useless Mantle on a short
fly, but Furillo walks and up bombs a game-winning grand slam

into the upper deck!
CRD 100 020 000 1 - 4 10 0
MDM 000 100 101 4 - 7 9 0
W-Purkey L-Roberts
HRS: Crandall, Furillo-2
GWRBI-Furillo

MASTERS 9, BIG FLIES 2

Yeah, our game was pretty darn easy by comparison. Cunningham lines a clutch two-run single in the 1st off Russ Meyer, Gus Bell singles, walks and smashes two homers to knock in four, and Bob Rush has little trouble with the wingless Big Fly lineup, Randy Jackson being their lone threat with a double, single and homer.
LBF 000 100 010 - 2 8 1
MOS 200 500 11x - 9 10 1
W-Rush L-Meyer
HRS: Jackson, Bell-2, Thomas
GWRBI-Cunningham
INJURY: R. Wilson-5

CLOCKERS 9, CAPS 0

In an even more predictable massacre, Johnny Schmitz throws a 3-hit shutout and the Clocker bats whale away on Billy Loes and two Coonskin "relievers" to keep themselves relevant in the Ozzie & Harriet. Loes, by the way, since coming over from the Bikini Bombs and replacing Gromek in the Caps rotation, is 1-6 with a 10.32 E.R.A., allowing 74 hits in 34 innings.
CPS 000 000 000 - 0 3 1
CLK 203 040 00x - 9 13 1
W-Schmitz L-Loes
HR: Hemus
GWRBI-Hemus

SUMMITEERS 9, MENACE 6

In what looks to be as lopsided a win as those last two for a while, the K2s jump out to a 7-0 lead on Vern Thies, when Nixon

and the wretched K2 pen start giving it all back. It's a three-run
game in the 9th with the tying run at the plate until Frank Smith
relieves Parnell and gets Ennis and Carrasquel to finish the Men-
ace off and give the Summits their 60th win the hard way.
RED 000 000 321 - 6 11 2
K2S 001 150 20x - 9 14 0
W-Nixon L-Thies SV-Smith
HRS: Majeski, Mathews-2 (#43,44)
GWRBI-Majeski

DARK FOOTSTEPS BEHIND ME AND US

I had to take three different cabs out to Grace Kelly's house
last night to keep Don Bollweg and Mike Blyzka from following
me. Frank Thomas went 3-for-4 and was so peeved the Masters
didn't win he "hired" two of our team lowlifes to rearrange my
face. Blyzka was all cocky because he relieved Liddle in the 8th
after the game was already lost, retired all six Big Flies he faced,
and wanted some kind of sick reward. Bollweg apparently was
just along for the fun.

It had to be somebody's fault, right? Lew Burdette, Randy
Jackson (two doubles) and Hank Bauer (two-run homer) were
off limits because they were the opposing team, so the ball-man
who was spending frequent evenings with the hitting coach was
the easiest target.

—"The boys just don't understand it," frowned Grace later over
her brandy glass, "Baseball breaks the hearts of six teams every
day. The way I see it, we're lucky to have seen less of those days
than anyone."

She was right of course, but at the rate the Bombs and
Flipsides were winning, that could soon change. Grace was a
lovely creature, and her coolness under fire may have been her
best feature. But in my experience just as a fan, the Baseball
Gods tend to not spare nobody.

I'M TOO YOUNG FOR THIS

Okay. It was time for the Masters to stop blaming me and Grace for their run of rotten luck. How about GM Thelma Ritter, or bench coach Jimmy Stewart, or owner Alfred Hitchcock, who's never around? Grace had the boys belting balls early, when they turned around a two-run Bauer homer with a Gus Bell solo shot, singles by Sauer and Thomas off Maglie, a Cunningham double and two-run shot by Ray Katt, and it was 5-2 for the home nine right away. Herm Wehmeier settled down for us for three innings, but then Bauer socked another homer with two aboard to tie the game.

Cunningham's homer off Hal Brown now put us back up 6-5, but then for two indescribable innings, as soon as Tremel took the hill with McDonald unavailable, we were covered in Big Flies faster than a rotting cadaver—and I put the blame on pitching coach Ray Milland and the vengeful Lord above. A two-out Hodges walk in the 7th, followed by a single and error on Adams and Jackson single [on a 1-3 chance] put the Flies up

Home of 1954 Freaks League Baseball

OZZIE & HARRIET DIVISION				RICKY & LUCY DIVISION			
Flipsides	68	47	—	Suspense Masters	68	48	—
Blackboard Seven	65	52	4	Bikini Bombs	65	50	2.5
Clock Rockers	63	53	5.5	K2 Summiteers	62	53	5.5
Red Menace	54	62	14.5	Marilyn DiMaggios	53	63	15
Chrome Derbies	54	65	16	B.Lagoons Matter	48	68	20
Lord of Big Flies	50	66	18.5	Coonskin Caps	47	70	21.5

Ballantine Beer watches your belt line
—with inner whistles from our often leading fact

GAMES OF SUNDAY, AUGUST 11TH				
BBS	9	LBF	15	
BKB	10	MOS	6	
RED	2	CRD	2	
K2S	5	MDM	5	
CPS	2	FLP	4	
CLK	13	BLM	2	
		★Star of the Day★		
		BOB SKINNER		

7-6. The top of the 8th was so long and horrible I left the field, changed into my street clothes and tried sitting in the stands to change the jinxes but after a walk, Ted Lepcio(!) homer, walk, single, wild pitch, walk, single, triple, single with another Adams error, and two more singles, the score was 15-6, matching the beating the Flipsides gave the Lagoons just yesterday, and the few Masters fans left in the stands realized who I was and were kicking me to the exit tunnel.

Sure, Grace is still excited because the Flipsides are here to-morrow to start a three-game set having won eight in a row, but there's one thing she might've missed: they now have a better record than the Masters do.

NOT EVEN SAUER POWER CAN HELP US

Hank Sauer took some pity on me when no one else would, and gave my back a real rubbing with his bat before the game. And wham! There went homer number 40 into the seats to give the Masters a 2nd inning run against George Zuverink after the dreaded Flipsides had opened the game with two off Mike Garcia. Bottom of the 6th, still 2-1 them, Garcia walked, Bell doubled with one out, Thomas tied the game with a single and Hank untied with a moon shot for homer #41! It was 5-2 us with Garcia primed for his fifteenth win. Easy right?

Not against a Flips squad that had won eight straight and just swept the Lagoons across town. Not against a team that had already benefitted from three lucky hits [two 1-5 chances and a 1-4] in the game. So Yost got himself plunked to begin the 7th, scored on a two-out single by Kiner that tired out Garcia, and another bullpen parade was a given. With McDonald need-ing one more day of rest, Garcia was left out there for the 8th but Frazier stung him for a solo blast to cut it to 5-4. Southpaw Chet Nichols came in to face lefties Fox, Snider, and Slaughter in the 9th, but the Duke crushed homer #31 to tie it up!

After Bil Tremel went one and two thirds scoreless innings and Jim Wilson retired all seven Masters he faced, Kinder came on to get pinch-hitter Agganis in the 10th. Harry walked, Adams doubled him to third, and we were a mere bingle away from taking the opener. But Kinder struck out Bell and Thomas and this one went to eleven. When with the same three Flippin' lefties due up, Bromo Seltzer was handed out to all 37,000 fans and lefty Chuck Stobbs took the mound. Fox, Snider, and Slaughter all singled [not one of the hits on Chuck's card], and Mike Blyzka was hailed to escape the mess. Minutes later, after we could do nothing with Kinder again, it was over.

The Flips' 69th win was also their ninth straight and 24th in their last 28, and the Suspenser locker room was a circle of hell afterwards. Joe Cunningham threatened to stuff me in a trash can and roll me down Bedford Avenue if another player touched me with his bat. I was so upset I ran across to the Flipside clubhouse and asked if I could be their ballboy, but Yost and Al Dark told me to take a hike. I was certainly in no mood to listen to Grace Kelly's hopeful malarkey again, but then she pulled me aside in a shadowy stadium corridor before I left.

—"Please don't give up on me or the team, Paulie. Not today and definitely not tomorrow."

"Why? What makes tomorrow so special? You think we're going to beat Lou Kretlow? I bet we couldn't even beat Bob Keegan right now!"

—"Because tomorrow Hitch will be in town. And you're expected at his 55th birthday party."

PARTY GOES OFF WITH A HITCH

"Good eeevening," said Hitchcock the second he got to the microphone last night at the Hotel Bossert in Brooklyn. Their famous Colorama Ballroom was illuminated by over a thousand multicolor bulbs, and there must have been a hundred people on hand, mostly team officials and players but also a fair number of famous notables like Mayor Wagner, Governor Dewey, Sid Caesar, Marlon Brando, and Ingrid Bergman. We were all there for a four-course dinner and massive birthday cake to be wheeled in for Alfred. Jimmy Stewart presented him with a giant auto-graphed baseball from the players, and Ray Milland led a rendi-tion of "For He's a Jolly Good Absentee Owner".

Now they say celebrities always look shorter in real life than you imagine they are, but Hitch was actually bigger and fatter, and a crack-up from start to finish.

"I want to thank you all for attending my 55th year in life's captivity. And especially to the Masters of Suspense for surviving their harrowing encounter earlier against the so-called Flipsides."

An army of waiters then came in and filled our fancy glasses with what looked like blue champagne.

"Pardon my impulsive jocularity," continued Hitch, lighting a fat cigar, "but a woman standing beside me in an elevator recent-ly turned to her friend and asked, 'Why is there no blue food? What have they done with all the blue food?' So I thought a humorous little experiment was in order. Enjoy your dinner." The same waiters then carried in the food: Waldorf salads, T-bone steaks, baked potatoes soaked in butter and sour cream—every single item drenched in deep blue food coloring. The gathering practically gasped in unison.

Hitch went to the far end of the table and sat, smoked his cigar without eating, and watched everyone struggle to swal-low their blue courses without getting sick. He was apparently delighted enough about the game's outcome earlier to carry through with his insane prank, and Grace Kelly, whose ear he whispered and laughed into pretty often, was safe in her hit-ting coach job for the time being. She asked me if I wanted to meet him but I said not this time, mostly because I was too busy enjoying the blue gin and tonics I had ordered.

Afterwards, George Burns helped wheel in a giant blue chocolate birthday cake which Gracie Allen popped out of. I'm telling ya, famous rich people can be nuts, but hanging around with 'em can be pretty fun.

NATIONAL UNLIKELY HEROES DAY

The names don't exactly drip off your tongue—Ralph Beard, Bob Keegan, Ted Lepcio, Billy Hunter, Matt Batts—but all of them played a special part in the day's shenanigans. In our big season series finale with the Flipsides, a mystery starter was given the ball due to Clem Labine's rotation crumminess, and boy did Ralph's Beard ever shine, throwing seven 4-hit shutout innings before Mr. Labine came on and blanked the Flips for the final two to make us the first team to 70 wins.

As for the offense, me and Grace were good luck charms once again, because Bobby Adams started our 1st with a line shot into the left field seats, added two walks and a triple later, the White Hurt singled and doubled and McDougald popped another homer with a man aboard in the 8th off Kinder. Now it's on to Cincinnati to face the Big Flies again, who skunked us twice when they were here, and I wager the poker playing and beer drinking will be back in force on that train.

BOTTOMS UP!

If you ask me, there's nothing more dangerous than a ball team that has a full day off when they get to a new city. The booze and poker games on the train carried us right into Cincinnati, where I spent most of the day with Brideweser and half of our roster at Mecklenburg Gardens in the Over-the-Rhine district,

eating sausages and drinking flagons of beer that were so foamy
you could water ski on them. At one point I had to take a break
from the sudsy doings and oom-pah-pah music and get the score
of the only game going from this guy's radio out on the street.
Luckily, it was being played up the Ohio road at Windy Gap
Park in Cleveland, so the K2 radio announcer was loud and clear,
and pretty disappointed...

TORTURE AFTER MIDNIGHT

The Over-the-Rhine district was out of the question after last
night's fiasco of a game. So was any kind of post-game dinner.
That's because Grace Kelly, sickened by the Masters offense
against a Big Flies hurler who had lost seven of his last eight de-
cisions (Sal Maglie), had learned about the endless beer-quaffing
on our day off and kept the players on the field until well-past
midnight, screeching at everyone who got into the batting cage
like either a siren or a harpy.

"You think that was a fastball, McDougald?? That was a powder puff compared to the one Meyer will throw at your chin
tomorrow! Get back in there if you call yourself a man!!"

I was the one throwing them weak fastballs, but being one of
the Over-the-Rhine imbibers myself, I ran out of gas after six or
seven batters and she swapped me out with Mike Blyzka.

It was grueling, and no one had ever seen this scary side of
Grace, but boy did we deserve it after Don Liddle pitched like a
piñata earlier and a Bobby Adams solo homer in the 7th was the
only offense we could muster in friendly Crosley Crush Field. A
double by Andy Pafko (who went 4-for-4) and triple by Randy
Jackson scored their first run, a Bauer homer their second, and
then after Cunningham flubbed a two-out grounder in the 5th,
ever-disappointing Gil Hodges cleared the bases with a triple for
three unearned runs. Two singles and a walk in the 6th knocked

out Liddle and brought in a trio of bullpen clowns, and with the Bikinis edging the Flips, our lead had shrunk to two and a half games again.

THOMAS AND SAUER AND THE REDEMPTION HOUR

I couldn't supply the home plate ump at Crosley Crush Field with new baseballs fast enough, because after their jock straps got pulled over their heads by Grace Kelly the night before, the Master batters hit nearly everything they saw out of sight against poor Russ Meyer. Hank Sauer blasted homers 42 and 43 his first two times up and singled later to knock in four, his partner in power crime Frank Thomas singled four times and doubled, and the Adams-Morgan Bobbys reached base eight out of eleven times combined. Mike Garcia, against the righty-heavy Big Fly lineup, rocked them to sleep on just five hits, over three times less safeties than we had. It was nice to see Gil McDougald doing his little Scottish jig in the clubhouse later, and it'll be nice to be done with these Flies after tomorrow, because they've been a pain in our posterior all year. Also, the timing couldn't have been better to locate our offense again, seeing we're off to Detroit next to face the smoking hot Clockers.

NOBODY KNOWS NOTHING, DOES ONE?

Just when things look positively cheery and hopeful, baseball's got this way of sneaking up on you from behind and whacking your head with a big wet sock. And not just our heads…

CAPS 11, CLOCKERS 1
To win their lucky thirteenth in a row, all the Clocks have to do is finish their season series with the Coonskins in Boston by

beating them for the 11th time in 12 games. And with Pascual and Conley locked up 1-1 into the 5th, it seems very possible. Which is when Gilliam and Smith walk, Fain blasts a homer into the bullpen, Wilson walks, and when Kemmerer relieves Camilo, Aaron and Shantz double, and the second of two Courtney passed balls in the inning bring home run number six. Four late runs off Corky Valentine are just for show, Conley ends up with a complete game five-hitter, and the Clockers slink back to Detroit to await the Masters.

CLK 001 000 000 - 1 5 0
CPS 100 060 31x - 11 13 1
W-Conley L-Pascual
HRS: Fain, Jones
GWRBI-Fain
INJURY: Fain-1
Clockers win season series 10-2

BOMBS 6, FLIPSIDES 0

All set to take advantage of the first Clocker loss in two weeks, the Flips get roadside Bombed and whitewashed by ex-Coonskin ace Steve Gromek, who improves to 16-5 by stranding nine and inducing three twin killings. The Bikini bats are just as methodical, scoring one run in six separate innings, including their last five in a row to build a heck of a picket fence.

FLP 000 000 000 - 0 7 0
BKB 010 111 11x - 6 12 0
W-Gromek L-Zuverink
HR: Boone
GWRBI-Boone

BIG FLIES 7, MASTERS 2

And yup, you guessed it. Our weekend in the Hell called Cincinnati ends with Rush serving up meatballs to Bauer, Hodges and the immortal Jack Dittmer, and the Flies swat our behinds for the fourth time in five games, this time by five runs while leaving ZERO runners on base. Duane Pillette, who pitches good enough to win nearly every time out, scatters nine hits, two by Rush himself, but gets plenty of offensive help for a change. Hate to tell ya this, but these Suspensers are a pretty ordinary 38-36 since May 26th, which is why our lead has shrunk to two and a half again. If they play like this in Detroit and Baltimore I may have to ride home in the luggage car.

MOS 010 000 010 - 2 9 0
LBF 003 001 30x - 7 6 0
W-Pillette L-Rush
HRS: Cunningham, Bauer, Hodges, Dittmer
GWRBI-Hodges
Flies win season series 7-5

SUMMITEERS 3, BLACKBOARDS 1

So all three Ozzie & Harriet contenders lose. Willard Nixon walks six guys in Cleveland but allows four hits and gets the win over the Seven when Mel Parnell relieves him in the ninth with one out and two aboard and Dale Mitchell is swapped out for Bob Nieman, who pinch-hits into a game-ending double play. The K2s sock three solo shots off Ned Garver, the go-ahead clout by Nixon himself!

BBS 100 000 000 - 1 4 1
K2S 002 100 00x - 3 5 1
W-Nixon L-Garver SV-Parnell
HRS: Mele, Nixon, Mathews (#47)
GWRBI-Nixon

DERBIES 7, DiMAGGIOS 3

As Jack Webb said later to a female reporter, "Just the blasts, ma'm." That would be a pair of two-run dingers by Bill Bruton and numbers 36 and 37 by Kluszewski in a very rare display of Derby power at Gasoline Alley off Porterfield. Mantle gets himself out of his drunk bed with a single and homer off Coleman and Furillo singles three times but never scores, as another day ticks off the second division calendar for these fellahs.

MDM 000 102 000 - 3 7 0

CRD 000 043 00x - 7 13 1
W0Coleman L-Porterfield
HRS: Mantle, Bruton-2, Klu-2
GWRBI-Bruton
DiMaggios win season series 7-5

LAGOONS 14, MENACE 1

Ah yes, the final big wet sock of the day, a pleasant little 5-1 lead over Harry Dorish and the Menace through six innings that turns into a mauling when the Lagoons score nine times off Miller, Spahn, Fowler, and Trotsky the Menace mascot in the 7th inning, the highlights being a three-run Eddie Waitkus homer off Spahnie and a Musial grand salami off Fowlie. John Antonelli is the beneficiary of the onslaught, and continues his weird season, dropping his E.R.A. to 2.82 and leading the league in whiffs but also near or at the top in walks and home runs allowed.

RED 000 100 000 - 1 7 0
BLM 022 100 90x - 14 17 0
W-Antonelli L-Dorish
HR: Rhodes (#38), Waitkus, Musial (#35)
GWRBI-Sarni

THESE ARE THE GAMES THAT TEST MEN'S INNARDS

I'm not a big fan of Detroit. The weather is sticky and buggy in August, the tavern choices aren't great, and from the second we entered our hotel lobby we were hounded by Clockheads, the ravenous fans of the Clock Rockers, who had just surged back into the Ozzie & Harriet pennant race with a 12-game win streak. The Rock Shop was deafening all afternoon, and even when Brideweser and me were laying in our beds later we could hear them singing their Bill Haley anthems in the street outside.

And on this first night they had good reason to, because their comeback and our latest loss was so unnerving it made me want to find Grace and escape over the Canadian border with her. Lefty Alex Kellner knocked Hank Sauer out for the series by plunking him in the very 1st inning, but we exploded in the 3rd with a McDougald single, Bell walk, and back to back upper deck shots by the White Hurt and Bobby Hofman! It was still 4-1 us in the 6th when the currently scorching Teddy Ballgame got mad and hit a solo shot off Wehmeier. He did the same thing off him in the 8th and it was 4-3.

Meantime, our bats went in the deep freeze after that third inning, with a Ray Katt single our only hit the rest of the game. After McCall shut us down, Wilhelm did the same in the 8th despite two walks and a wild pitch. In the 9th, Agganis batted for Hofman and reached on an error. Katt then slugged one toward the stands with two outs but Williams leaped and snatched away a two-run homer! Jim McDonald then came on to save our day and had absolutely nothing. He beaned Lloyd Merriman (to knock him out of action for the series), walked Hatfield, and Courtney tied it up at five with a clean double. Logan walked to load the bases. Cass Michaels batted for WIlhelm and hit into a force at home plate, but pesky Richie Ashburn ripped a single and we'd barfed away a big one!

MY KIND OF TOWN!

Detroit is a gas, man. There's Woodward Avenue, and bustling auto factories, and the cool houses along Lake St. Clair in Grosse Pointe, and the Institute of Arts, and when we shut up the Clocker fans for a day with a last-minute comeback at the Rock Shop, all is good.

No doubt that our teams are evenly matched right now. Morgan and McDonald both club solo homers off Johnny Schmitz but another two-run upper deck job by torrid Ted Williams has us in a 2-2 tie. Ralph Beard is less effective than he was last time out, though, and three Clocker singles put them up 3-2 after four. With Sauer out with his big owie, Gus Bell fills in with an RBI double in the 6th and Katt's sac fly puts us back up 4-3. Katt then has a defensive inning from hell in the 7th, letting two passed balls get by him with people aboard against Labine and helping the Clocks score twice to put them back up 5-4. With Schmitz going for a complete win in the 9th, Don Bollweg leads with a pinch double. Morgan grounds out but when Wilhelm enters, his knuckleball ain't knucklin'. McDougald gets plunked, Adams bats for Hoak and singles to load the bases, White Hurt whiffs but Cunningham hits for Hofman and walks in the tying run. Then Bell walks, McDonald doesn't pitch like crap for a change and we eek out the win! Two exciting games in a row with these guys, with Garcia pitted against Sullivan in today's finale.

GETTNG CROWDED AT OZZIE & HARRIET'S AGAIN

Grace and me managed to stay away from each other in Detroit because the Clocker games were too crucial and we didn't want to upset the team's apple cart. But she did set up a cute little system to pass notes back and forth during the last game, where a pimply Rock Shop helper ran back and forth from the club level to our dugout, and a fresh note was waiting for me every time I came off the field.

—*GARCIA LOOKS STINKY TODAY* was her first one.
THAT AIN'T GOOD said me. YOU GOING TO BALTIMORE WITH THE TEAM?
—*SADLY NO. WILL VISIT MY PARENTS AGAIN IN PHILADELPHIA.*
(Not sadly for me, seeing I wasn't invited back to that stuffy mausoleum.)

HOPE SAUER IS BACK FOR THAT SERIES. OUR OF-
FENSE IS A FEW EGGS SHORT OF AN OMELETTE.
   —*WHAT ARE YOU TALKING ABOUT?*
   NEVER MIND. IT'S TOO HOT TODAY AND THE BOT-
TOM OF MY WOOL UNIFORM KEEPS GIVING ME A
RASH IN A PLACE I DON'T WANT TO TELL YOU.
   —*THEN PLEASE DON'T. MAYBE WE CAN ESCAPE FOR
A DINNER OUT FOLLOWING THE GAME?*
   I CAN HANDLE THAT, BUT IT'LL BE A LOT SAFER
IF WE WIN.

SAME AS THEY EVER WAS

It was a relaxing, highball-enhanced, all-night train ride for me
from Milwaukee to Baltimore, with no Grace Kelly or needy teammates to get in my ear. I read a *Sporting News* front to back, then at
least a third of this weird funny novel called "Catcher in the Rye"
(which wasn't about baseball, if you can believe it), before I finally
passed out somewhere across Ohio. As far as the day's games went,
the weird thing is that with all the Ozzie & Harriet clubs losing
except the Big Flies and all the Ricky & Lucys winning except the
Caps, the tight three-team races didn't budge an inch...

FEELING CRABBY ALL OVER AGAIN

It may have been easier if my train had overshot the Baltimore
station and dumped me in Chesapeake Bay. Another winnable
game for us became a loss thanks to Roy Sievers, who batted
cleanup against lefty Liddle and powered a three-run homer in
the 1st to put us behind the 8-ball all afternoon, then added a
sac fly two innings later after a Lollar single and Kuenn double
for his fourth ribbi. It was 5-1 Chromers following a Wally Post

bomb, catcher Red Wilson tripped on a pebble and knocked himself out for a week to add to the fun, before two late rallies against Joe Coleman and Bob Greenwood fell a run short. It was even more infuriating for the team seeing that the Bikini Bombs had the day off, and inched to just one game behind in the loss column again. Because we won the opener with me out in Milwaukee, no one would talk to me afterwards, though from what I saw no one was talking to anybody, with Robin Roberts looming for us in the series finale.

SHEER HELL IN OZZIE & HARRIET'S HOUSE

After I got back from our close win in Baltimore today I met up with Bobby Z. and Donny Gold for late burgers and a few games of bowling in Great Neck, but to tell ya the truth I'm getting a little bored with them, because all they ever wanna hear about are details of my times with DiMaggio and Grace. I tried to steer the subject to Bobby's latest summer job working a balloon-popping booth at Coney Island, or to Donny Gold's experience working for his TV wholesaler pop, but no dice. I was tired from all my traveling and ball collecting during these sticky hot days, and after my third Rheingold I started guttering more bowling balls on purpose to get the last game over with so I could get home and enjoy my bed again. With the dreaded Clock Rockers coming to town next to play their final regular series with us, I needed a good sleep. Which I'm sure was more than any followers of the Ozzie & Harriet race got...

YIKES IS RIGHT: ANATOMY OF A CLOCKING

'Twas a beautiful warm Monday afternoon in Brooklyn. The Clock Rockers were in town to finish their season series with us after we'd just come off a close win down at Gasoline Alley. Grace Kelly was back in her club level suite entertaining the reporters. The Rear Window stands were packed solid. A brass band played on the dugout roof before the game. White fleecy clouds floated over the yard, and the smells of cigars and frankfurters were in the air...

And then our asses were handed to us via special delivery. Believe it or else, Mike Garcia had a 4-2 lead entering the 6th with the help of a big three-run bomb by Joe Cunningham off Sullivan in the 4th. From that point on, the Clockers pulverized six of our pitchers 13-2. After allowing ten hits and a third and fourth run to tie it in the 6th, Garcia tired rapidly in the 7th after a walk and two singles loaded the bases with no one out. When Campanella hit for Sullivan, Clem Labine came on and walked him to put the Clocks ahead. Chuck Stobbs tried his luck with the three lefties atop their lineup but Ashburn and Dee Fondy singled and Adams booted a ball for a fifth run. Chuck did get Ted Williams on a double play and then Skowron on a liner to end the mess, but then Bill Tremel gave up three more in the 8th, Mike Blyzka was blitzed for another three in the 9th without recording an out, and the never-seen Ted Gray had to get the final guys.

With the Bikini Bombs resting, the fiasco of a massacre put us even in the loss column with them, while the Clocks are now in a virtual tie for first with the also-idle Flipsides! Masters players fought in the clubhouse later, less over the game and more about who was going to get to knock over the food table. (As usual, Frank Thomas won.) Grace skirted me off to Oyster Bay again so we could drown our sorrows in gin, and around midnight she received an unsettling overseas call from London: Hitch would be in town for the rest of the series and he was not a jolly fellow.

SCRIPT-FLIPPERS STRIKE AGAIN

I'll get to the relatively entertaining Rear Window Stadium battle soon, but first this real masterpiece of suspense out in St. Louis…

FLIPSIDES 6, SUMMITEERS 5
Neither Dean Stone nor Sonny Dixon is at their best, and it's a back-and-forth 4-2 lead for the Flips into the 6th when a Runnels solo homer starts the inning, singles by Mele and Rivera follow, and Ellis Kinder is hailed from the pen. Stone, who homered earlier, bunts them over, and the K2s take the lead on a Robinson single and Abrams scoring grounder. In the last of the 7th, Andy Seminick bats for Kinder and gets himself plunked. Ed McGhee runs for him. Groth flies out but Yost triples in the tying run and sends Stone packing for Frank Smith. Kiner hits a deep sac fly to put the Flips back ahead and the action moves to the 9th against Don Mossi, whose appearances have been nothing short of ugly lately. He gets Vernon and Mathews easily, but Bob Cerv hits for Burgess and clubs one deep to right-center field…Duke Snider races to the wall, leaps at the last second and robs Cerv of a game-tying homer to end it! [A 1-rating in CF is always a good thing.] The razor-thin win puts the Flips a full game in front of the Clockers again.
K2S 001 103 000 - 5 11 3
FLP 003 010 20x - 6 8 1
W-Kinder L-Stone SV-Mossi
HRS: Stone, Runnels
GWRBI-Kiner

MASTERS 6, CLOCKERS 4
Yep, things look deja vu-ish for us when the Brocktonites plate four off Rush in the top of the 1st before the ushers even wipe the seats off. Except Bill Renna evens things in the bottom half with a grand salami off Herr Johnny Schmitz, and the

score stays frozen until the 5th, when a walk, single, and wild pitch give us the lead, and in the 7th, when White Hurt Thomas greets Hoyt "Not Himself Lately" Wilhelm with a solo blast, and Rush throws a dominating 4-hit shutout after that first inning to become our first 20-game winner! It would be nice if the Bikinis would lose for a change, but hell, we'll take it.

CLK 400 000 000 - 4 8 0
MOS 400 010 10x - 6 8 0
W-Rush L-Schmitz
HRS: Renna, Thomas

WE GET THE DAY OFF THE BIKINIS WISH THEY HAD

I mean, seriously? With lefties Dick Littlefield and Billy Hoeft slated in Milwaukee, the Bombs just need another win against the second division Menace to inch to a half game behind the idle Masters again. So of course after scoring once in the 1st, Hoeft shuts them out the final eight innings. And of course pairs of hits from Carrasquel, Avila, and Ennis are enough for the injury-marred Commies to edge them by one run again. If the Bikinis end up losing the race by one game, they'll remember these two cold days at Marx Field.

FROM THE HIGHEST PEAK TO THE DARKEST DEPTHS

While I was trying to sneak my way out to the street after our latest debacle of a loss, one of the clubhouse helper guys grabbed my arm and stuffed a note in my pocket.

—"This guy just called looking for ya. I wrote down his info."

"Who was it?"

—"Hey, I ain't your secretary. Somebody named Joe." He ducked back inside and I opened the note:

MACK'S ALL-NIGHTER LOUNGE
248 Front St.
soon as you can

Mack's was a sad Manhattan watering hole just over the Brooklyn Bridge and in the shadow of the thing. A juke box played Billie Holiday and the place was almost empty except for a few colored guys having beers.

Joe DiMaggio sat by himself at the bar, maybe on his third Gibson, an ashtray stuffed with cigarette butts in front of him. He had a rumpled overcoat on, hadn't shaved in a while, and the old colored barkeep didn't even seem to recognize him. Heck, I barely did. He gave me a boozy hug when I took the stool next to him, and then ordered me a Gibson even though I said I'd be happy with a ginger ale.

—"Just wanted to tell ya, Paul…That's you've done everything I asked ya to do, meaning with those Masters, but this race is over now. It's cooked like Mama's manicotti."

"That's not true. The Bombs are still in second place and the K2s don't got the pitching—"

—"I mean for us, Paul. For us. Fifteen back with thirty to go? Ha!" He grabbed the pickled onion from his empty glass and mashed it in his teeth. "Never should've signed that bum kid Mantle. Still hitting .241 and today the Clockers even walked Billy Goodman to pitch to him with two aboard and the dope grounds out again. Know what? I think he drinks too much…" He waved to the barkeep for a fourth Gibson. "Anyway, reason I got ya down here, is to say…that I officially release you from your service to Joseph Paul DiMaggio. You wanna help them Masters win and marry Grace Kelly, that's okay with me."

"Cripes. You know about her too?"

—"Who the hell doesn't? Just tell me: Has she been worth it?"

"Well…so far. I guess—"

—"Because I'm hitched to Marilyn, and that nutty famous broad's been worth nothin' but indigestion. Tried to talk her out of makin' this stupid new comedy and take a break from the acting baloney but she won't hear it. Matter of fact she'll be out here next month doing a big scene or two from it and getting the press on her every move and I gotta answer dumb questions about her for weeks on end—" He laid his drunk head on my shoulder. "I dunno if I can do it anymore, kid. She's draining me."

My drink arrived and I took one mind-numbing sip. Nudged his head off my shoulder.

"Don't worry Joe. Just stay frosty with everything. Things'll work out. Back in the 1930s and 40s? You were just the coolest ballplayer on the field. Everything you did out there. My Pop watched you all the time and he told me that."

—"He did?"

"Yeah. Life throws us curveballs we don't expect, so we just gotta be ready to either let 'em go by, or whack 'em."

He nodded, crushed out his latest cigarette.

—"All those pennants and awards I won, and I gotta go to some Brooklyn kid for marriage advice. What would I do without you, Paul?"

"Uhhh. Live above Mack's All-nighter Lounge?"

He nodded and smiled, revealing his big teeth, then began laughing, and didn't know how to stop.

TAKE THAT! AND THAT!!

Ralph Beard had another unexpectedly great start, allowing a Clockers run in the 1st due to his own error before shutting them out the next four and a third innings. Clem Labine came on to finish the 6th with two aboard, then threw a 1-2-3 7th, getting Ashburn, Fondy, and Williams on easy flies. For us, Bobby Morgan stroked his fourth miracle homer [on a 1-5 chance] of the week, and in the 5th, Tom Brewer soiled himself and had to flee to the showers after Bell doubled, Thomas homered after a wild pitch, and Cunningham followed with another blast. It was 5-1 Masters. I peered up at Grace's suite and saw Hitch kissing her hand and bidding her farewell to get back across the ocean to further storyboard meetings for "To Catch a Thief". All was right with the Suspensers' world.

Which was when dark storm clouds drifted over the ballpark, thunder could be heard, and Rear Window Stadium's roof caved in. Walks to Skowron and Hatfield began the top of the 8th. Westlake put one in the left field seats and it was 5-4. Jim Mc-Donald rushed in early from the pen but Courtney singled. He got Logan on a liner but Cass Michaels batted for relieverer Kemmerer and knocked one in the same seats [on a 1-4 chance] for a 6-5 Clockers lead! McDonald calmed himself down, got Ashburn, but Fondy singled, Williams singled, Skowron hit one to New Rochelle and eight winning runs were across. We died against Wilhelm in our 8th and 9th without a murmur, I took the liberty of turning over the food table myself before one player could slink into the clubhouse, and our worst loss of the year by far was history. Pop even gave me a sympathy hug when I got home. I realized I was still getting paid by Joe to help this team lose, but their drawn-out sad plight had been growing on me. At least we'd get the beatable (I think) Chrome Run Derbies next.

CARDBOARD INSPIRATION, PAULIE-STYLE

Feeling a little liberated and jazzed up from my cocktail with DiMaggio the night before, I found a piece of white cardboard in the locker room before tonight's game, scrawled a big message on it in capital letters and propped it on the food table for all the players to see:

IT'S THE FRIGGIN' CHROME DERBIES, FOR CRIPES SAKES! COME ON, GUYS!!!

The "cripes" gave it away that it was me, and everyone,

including Frank Thomas, went back to rubbing their bats or gloves on my back when they took the field for pre-game practice.

And then Curt Simmons paid the price. After Garcia got the Derbs 1-2-3 in the top of the 1st, Hoak singled, McDougald walked, Sauer singled, the White Hurt singled home two, and after Hofman and Katt grounded out, Renna mashed a three-run shot into the upper deck and the game was ours. Morgan added another in a series of recent dingers later, Garcia's only pimples were a double, homer, and walk by Hobie Landrith, and I had a juicy steak from Peter Luger's coming my way later.

BITTERSWEET AND WAY TOO SAUER

September was on top of us, and we were nine outs away from losing two of three to the fourth place Chromers and dropping into second place because the Bikini Bombs were throttling the Flips again. With both catchers hurt, good old Hank Sauer strapped on the gear, but Joe Coleman had our number and Bill Bruton was running wild on Bob Rush. He walked twice, singled once, stole three bases to make him 13-0 doing that, and scored both Derby runs on Harvey Kuenn singles.

Cunningham began our 7th with a clean double and Renna walked. Morgan whiffed but a passed ball [on a "1" chance] advanced the runners. Rush whiffed but McDougald walked, loading the sacks for Mr. Sauer and his sore knees.

But guess what? His arms weren't. The first pitch from Coleman went about as far as a ball could go without being picked up on Air Force radar. The grand slam was dinger #45 for Hank and gave us a huge 4-2 win to keep us in first place! Afterwards, I was so ecstatic I scribbled a personal note to Sauer and slid it into his locker:

Dear Hank:

What you did today in the bottom of the 7th was so heroic, especially in a game we had to win and in a game in which you were a catcher for the first time. You've just been so reliable, and if we end up winning the pennant I'll sure remember this one today. You make me proud to be a ballboy—I mean man.

—Paulie

He was still out on the field talking to reporters, so I didn't wait around to see his reaction. Instead I walked home and picked up some Italian sausages and fresh bread for Mama on the way.

What I didn't expect was to see Hank waiting for me at the front steps of our apartment building. He wasn't smiling at all. Grabbed me with his meaty hands and shoved me into the adjoining alley.

"What's the matter??" I cried.

—"How about this?" he barked, and took out the note I stuck in his locker. "You think I'm stupid? A dopey home run hitter who isn't gonna recognize handwriting I know I've seen before?"

"What are you talking about?"

—"The note you dropped in the front seat of my car, you weasel. 'Reliable information from a reliable source'? That Grace Kelly is a Commie?"

Oh crap, I thought. I used the word reliable in both notes and my Rs have a distinct flip on the end.

—"That one you left that pumped up the team yesterday got me thinking. And this one confirms everything. Who you been spying for? The Bikinis? The Summiteers?"

"Actually…DiMaggio hired me. And it hasn't exactly helped him."

—"Who woulda thunk it? A ballboy traitor. Right in our midst."

"I know. It was dumb. But please don't tell Mr. Hitchcock about this, okay? And definitely not Grace,"

—"Don't worry, weasel. Like you, I don't like to see her upset."

He finally let go of me, pointed a big finger at my nose.

—"But if I see you within an inch of our clubhouse again, I'll not only rearrange your bone structure, I'll get Thomas to help me do it with his bat."

He marched off, making sure to crush the wrapped sausages that fell on the sidewalk. I resumed breathing. My mind was already scrambling about what I would say to Grace…

RE-TOOLING ON A COUCH IN QUEENS

Because Bobby Z. was in Cleveland reporting on last night's game and I was afraid to have to face Pop and explain why I didn't have my job with the Masters anymore, I hopped a bus out to Queens and took a couch in Vin Pascarelli's basement. Vin threw dice with me and Bobby and Donnie and Luther sometimes and lived with his folks and worked at his dad's muffler shop on Union Turnpike and he was a serious greaser with an unsmoked cigarette behind each ear and always drank the worst beer.

—"So what the hell ya gonna do now? " he asked, "And what's DiMaggio like?"

"Right now he's drinking too much. But forget about him. I gotta figure out how to tell Grace about this."

—"What's she like?"

"Vin. You gonna help me or what?"

He slid out one of his ear cigs, lit up and popped a new one in its place.

—"Maybe it ain't what you tell her, it's what you do."

"Huh?"

—"Chicks love romance, right? Gettin' swept off their feet and stuff. Maybe you can get out of town on a little vacation and take her with ya, do the flowers and wine and hotel thing—"

"Yeah, how? On a bus?"

—"Relax Paulie, I'm gettin' there. See, I know this guy named Jack who's got a nice '52 Plymouth convertible he's trying to unload."

"Jack who?"

—"I dunno. Forgot his last name. He's from up in Massachusetts but is living in the city trying to become a big writer. He drove the thing into my dad's shop a month ago to get a new muffler but now he wants to hitchhike across the country and he's short on cash, so…"

"Hitchhike?"

—"Yeah. He's kind of a nut. Anyway, I can call him and we can meet him at the shop like tomorrow or the next day. Can you put your girlfriend off till then? She'll dig the wheels, no doubt. It's maroon and pretty sweet."

"Pretty sure she's got her own car."

—"Yeah, but this one'll show up with you behind the wheel, Paulie."

Vin had a point there. Now I just had to come up with the winning pitch.

TIME TO HIT THE ROAD, JACK

This guy Jack from Massachusetts whose last name was Kerouac was a character, alright. Wore jeans, a white T-shirt, loafers, and had his black hair slicked up with a little curl on top. Plus he talked like a mile a minute and I needed a translator.

—"Be good to Polly, brother, and she'll be good to you."

"Who's Polly?"

—"The Plymouth, brother, the Plymouth! Polly's short for Polyhymnia, the Greek Muse of sacred poetry, sacred hymn, sacred dance, and most important, eloquence. Polly rides smoother than an eloquent poet, regardless of where your roamings roam."

"That's hip. But how many miles per gal–"

—"24, Eleanor. Enough to get you and your muse as far as Detroit, if not St. Loo. Even got a radio that works, so you can pick up and entertain any stray vagabonds along the way that resemble me."

"You mean hitchhikers?"

"Yeah, but the friendly ones. Ones without beds, without coins, without food, happy to lay under the Dippers surrounded by gutter piss and drink their lives down the toilet, all the time wishing they'd done that thing, that supreme thing that could've saved them, saved them from watery soup and holy garments of stink, saved them from bad preachers, carnival barkers—

"JACK! Vin Pascarelli yelled, "Tell him how much you want for the car already!"

Jack shrugged. "Eh, nine hundred should do it. And you can pay me whenever."

What a guy! We shook hands on the deal, I promised to take care of his Polly, and then I parked her in the alley behind our apartment building and took Pop outside to impress him.

—"Where you going in that thing?"

"Don't exactly know yet. But I'm already thinking about it."

Grace, who far as I knew hadn't been told I was off the team, was out in Cleveland with the Masters, but would be back in town in a few days because the team had a series at the Pinstripe Lagoon next. That's when I'd drive out to Oyster Bay and pop the question I might have to come up with on the spot.

THE CLEVELAND CACCIATORE CALL

Well, I was planning on pulling up at Grace's house in Polly the Plymouth tomorrow, but she beat me to the punch by calling me from Cleveland right in the middle of Mama's brisket cacciatore.

—"What happened to you, sweetheart? Are you sick? None of

the players will tell me a thing."

"Er, it's a long story. There's a lot of other stuff going on in my life all of a sudden, and I'm uh, having what you might call a…'20s life crisis."

There was a long pause.

—"It's another girl, isn't it?"

"Not really. I mean her name is Polly, but you'll meet her tomorrow and I swear you'll understand everything."

—"Why would I want to meet another girlfriend, Paulie? What's wrong with you??"

"She's not a girl. Just trust me, okay? When will you be home?"

—"I don't know, maybe in the afternoon. The boys are taking the train and I'm flying, but who knows what the weather will do. And I wish you'd confess already about this hussy."

"Arrgh. Just forget it for now. Trust me. Is your game over?"

—"No, but we're winning 3-0 after six. That Hank Sauer has been quite the powder keg lately. He hit another home run tonight and he could end up with three of our last four game-winners. He won't say a word to me either, and I wish I knew what's gotten him going again."

"He's just a pro, Grace. They all are. Doesn't seem like those guys need me anyway, right?

—"Maybe. But I do, Paulie. Promise you will never do anything behind my back to hurt me, as long as we're together."

Oh cripes…

"I promise. Can I go finish my cacciatore now?"

—"Bon appetite, love."

MEANWHILE…

As she feared, Grace's plane got delayed a day due to thunderstorms, so I spent the time packing a suitcase and filling the trunk of the Plymouth with "snack bags" from Mama. Then I followed the crazy game of the day...

SUMMITEERS 9, DIMAGGIOS 7

Things looked bleak for the K2 nine after a series of bleakness with the Masters. Three walks and a two-base Rivera error in the 5th were followed by a Del Crandall grand slam, and Turley's 2-1 lead was turned into a 5-2 deficit. Like, big deal. A walk, Collins error, single, walk, walk, single, walk and two more singles off the once-effective Bob Lemon give the Summits seven runs in the bottom of the same inning, before the surprise pitching of Tex Clevenger (three shutout frames) and Frank Smith, who whiffs Crandall and gets Belardi on a fly with the tying runs at second and third ends the madness.

MDM 000 150 001 - 7 9 1
K2S 020 070 00x - 9 8 1
W-Turley L-Lemon SV-Smith
HR: Crandall
GWRBI-Robinson

SPLITTIN' THE SCENERY...

It was the best of timing and the worst of timing to drive Polly to Oyster Bay. Best because Bob Rush had thrown a one-hit shutout at the Lagoons in the afternoon, so I knew Grace was in a very positive mood. But bad because she whined and dined with the boys in Manhattan after the game in the Bronx and I found myself parked behind a tree down the road from her house for a good two hours waiting for her to finally show up later.

Finally her driver wheeled the Lincoln town car past me, churning up gravel dust, and I snapped out of my daydream. Checked my hair and snappy striped sport jacket in the mirror and cruised up her driveway to the front door. Rang the bell, a dozen roses in hand. One of her servants opened the door instead of her.

"Oh hi Floyd," I whispered, "Go get Grace for me."

—"Is she expecting you?"

"Of course not. Why ya think I'm whispering?"

He grumbled something and walked away. After what seemed like two minutes, Grace finally appeared at the door. Lovely as ever and still tipsy, thank God. Beamed and gasped and threw her arms around me.

"I want you to meet Polly," I said.

She froze and recoiled, looking over my shoulder.

"You brought that woman here??"

"It's my new car, Grace! Ain't she gorgeous?"

"Why did you buy a car?"

"Because I wanted to show-and-tell you why I left the team, rather then do it over the phone—"

—"You are just plain kooky, Paulie Rubin."

"Damn right I am. And listen. I don't know about you, but this baseball season is just thrilling the crap out of me. Problem was that being on the field collecting balls for the Masters day and night, I was only seeing 1/16th of it. And look, I know you got that new movie to make with Hitch when the season's over, so I thought, why don't we take a month-long baseball road vacation now and see as many of the big final games as we can? I mean… together."

She curled her lip and frowned.

—"Oh, but I have a job, Paulie. I'm their hitting coach and without me there—"

"They'll be fine. Hell, look what they did today without hardly hitting. Hank's back on track and even if they slump again you can talk to some of the hitters by phone from wherever we are, right?"

—"Wherever we are?"

"C'mere…"

I took her arm and walked her out to the convertible. Opened the passenger door and she paused, then slid onto the seat with her flowers, delighted and still mystified.

"Just imagine sailing along on an Ohio highway, not in any hurry to be anywhere, eat and spend nights where we want, no cares in the world. I'm getting goose bumps on my goose bumps already."

—"But Paulie, we need SOME kind of schedule for this—"

"Exactly!"

I yanked a little spiral notebook out of my jacket pocket, especially prepared for the moment.

"First we hit the Flipsides and Chrome Derbies in Baltimore, then the Clockers and Blackboards in Pittsburgh starting the 11th, then up to Beantown for the Bombs and Caps, then an extra day to drive out to St. Louis for the Clockers and Flips on the 17th, then—"

She shut me up by kissing me.

"This is too adventurous for me to resist, you sweet devil. But... will you let me drive her too?"

"Sure I will—"

She hopped out of the car with her flowers and yelled at the open front door.

"Floyd! Pack four of my bags!"

FIRST STOP: THE ATLANTIC

With another two days to go before our date with the Flipsides series in Baltimore, I agreed to let Grace's parents in Philly be our first road stop, but only if we spent the first day relaxing at the Jersey shore. So I cruised us south down the turnpike and then cut southeast toward the ocean. I knew Atlantic City would be too mobbed seeing this was the last weekend before a lot of beach places closed, and not wanting Grace to get recognized I kept going until we ended up in Wildwood—sort of a miniature Coney Island.

Grace had put on sunglasses and a head scarf like Marilyn had done, and luckily didn't have the bosomy figure to draw as many eyes. Neither of us brought bathing suits neither, so we just walked on the sand in our bare feet and shot a few rifles at a stuffed animal game (she won herself a big turtle) and rode on a coaster and ate crappy beach food and shared a bottle of wine until we fell asleep curled up in the open convertible in a big parking lot with stars and surf noise all around us.

"What excuse did you end up using to tell the team you were leaving?" I finally asked during an idle moment.

—"Oh, I didn't tell them anything. I've been taking off for occasional Hollywood meetings all year, so I assume they'll just think this is another one."

I stared at her. "A month-long meeting?"

—"You worry too much, Paulie. And like you said, if one of the hitters goes into a slump, I can always help him with a phone call."

Or if it's Hank and he decides to get blabby about that "Commie note" I wrote him, I wanted to say but was afraid to, I might just have a nervous breakdown instead...

YEAH, I HAD BETTER THINGS TO DO

My second visit with Grace's parents in their leafy suburb of Philly lasted all of one hour. That's how long it took for her dad to grill me with five dumb questions about my car and the route I was going to take (which I didn't exactly know yet), and then two or three more annoying questions from her mom about where we might be sleeping on the trip ("Don't you dare camp out!"). I mean geez, she was a grown woman with a good job and a bunch of Hollywood movies under her belt and she was being treated like a 16-year-old.

I kissed Grace and told her I'd be back later after I "bought a few things" for the trip, then drove into the city to visit the Liberty Bell, Independence Hall, the big art museum (which Grace would have like much more than me), dine on a fat cheesesteak in Rittenhouse Square, walk along the Schuylkill River and I even had time to take in a ballgame.

That's right, Connie Mack Stadium in the North End where the Phillies and Athletics were getting some time off was being used for a Negro League exhibition night game between the Detroit Stars and Indianapolis Clowns. That Henry Aaron kid on the Coonskins was on the Clowns team just a year ago, and they weren't missing him much, because according to the colored kids I was sitting with (being one of about three whites in the crowd of around 800), Indy had a win percentage way above .600, with the Memphis Red Sox, Birmingham Black Barons (where Willie Mays came from), Stars, Louisville Clippers, and K.C. Monarchs bringing up the rear of the Negro American League.

Cripes, could these players play. If only our TV networks would broadcast one of their games, I'm sure it would give the league a boost and keep it around for a while!

Anyway, I still wasn't ready to go back to the Kelly Mausoleum afterwards so found a smoky bookie joint down on South Street to get all the Freaks League details of the day. And did that ever eat up some time…

WITNESSES TO A CRIME, SORT OF

Well, the first game stop of our September motor trip turned out to be more memorable than we could have imagined. Grace didn't care for the light odor of petrol that permeated Gasoline Alley, but she did enjoy her Baltimore crabcake sandwich and cold foamy cup of National Bohemian. She was also entertained

by the polite welcome Chrome Derby skipper Jack Webb gave us
an hour before the game in the home dugout, even though every
time she asked why his team hadn't played better, he kept saying
"Just the stats, ma'm."

Then their opener against the third place Flipsides began, and
so did the real entertainment. Even though Grace was hiding
her fame well with dark glasses and a head scarf, we found seats
in a mostly empty section of the upper deck over home plate that
smelled a lot less gassy, and was a great place to watch Bob Feller
and Robin Roberts work their magic .

Except Roberts didn't have any, and two singles, a double,
and sac fly put the Flips ahead 3-0 out of the garage. A Bruton
single, Delsing double and Kuenn sac fly gave the Derbs one
back right away, but then that Feller fellah began cruising, and
allowed just one run his next six innings. After doubles from
Dark and Frazier in the 7th to make it 5-2 for the visitors, fans
started leaving and Grace started yawning and looking at her
nails. On the out-of-town scoreboard, her Masters were tied
1-1 with the Caps through six, but that didn't even seem to
interest her.

—"Can't we just take a ride around the harbor or something,
Paulie?"

"I never leave a game early, Grace. It's bad luck."

—"For who?"

"I don't know, it just is."

—"I don't believe in old wives or husbands tales. I'm going
down to the concourse to sneak into the ladies' room and hope-
fully restrain myself from another crabcake sandwich."

I said fine, then sat by myself and watched that Feller fellah fall apart faster than an Italian car. In a month of horrible
script-flipping by the Flips (now 2-6 in September), this had to
take the cake. Feller still had an 8-game win streak, had walked
no one and was six outs away from a 17-3 record when Delsing worked him for a leadoff walk. Kuenn singled, Kluszewski

singled to make it 5-2 and up stepped season-long under-
achiever Sid Gordon. Feller threw one weak fastball and Sid
drove it into the Pit Stop section of the left field bleachers for a
go-ahead home run! The few fans who were left went bonkers,
and after the Flips went out 1-2-3 against Greenwood in the
9th, Grace finally rushed back up to her seat.

—"What happened??"

"I'll tell you but you won't believe it."

—"Paulie? Don't ever let me go to the restroom in the 8th inning of a 5-2 game ever again."

"Deal."

FLIPS TRAPPED IN A WEBB AGAIN, AND THEY AIN'T ALONE

The way the Flipsides have been going this month, nothing
less would surprise me. With lefty Curt Simmons hurling for
the Chromers in Gasoline Alley, Al Dark was moved up to the
second spot, Gus Zernial was flexing his bat muscles and Jack
Shepard was slotted fifth. Dark even hit a rare homer in the 1st
inning to put them on the board first. So naturally by the 3rd
inning, the Derbies had scored four runs on five hits off Zuverink and Zernial was hit by a pitch and knocked out for the rest
of the series. And yeah, Simmons tucked them in bed the rest of
the way, handing the Flips their seventh loss in nine games this
month, and by the end of this thing even I was sitting there in
the upper deck looking at my nails.

"I think we should go drive around the harbor," I told Grace.

—"Oh no Paulie, let's take a nice stroll. We could use the
exercise."

And so we did, Grace clutching my arm and staying unrecog-
nized in her quiet disguise by the people who passed. The aroma
of seafood restaurants was everywhere. We talked about the next

stop on our road trip, a big two-game set in Pittsburgh between the Clock Rockers and Blackboard Seven.

But then we passed a newsstand, and a screaming headline on the back page of the out-of-town *New York World-Telegram*:

WHERE'S GRACE?
Famous Actress and Hitting Coach
"Missing" from Masters

"What the heck is this?" I nearly shouted at Grace, "Didn't you tell the team you were leaving?"

—"Why bother? I've left for movie business meetings all season, haven't I?"

"Yeah, but someone obviously checked up on that with Hitchcock! We're screwed!"

I bought a copy of the paper to pore over at the hotel. Or maybe it would be in the car, seeing we now had to split Baltimore and head to western Pennsylvania as soon as possible.

REPORTERS IN MY SOUP BOWL

Thankfully I had a thriller of a showdown game at Forbes Jungle Park to keep me occupied last night, because after seeing that New York newspaper headline about Grace being missing and me driving like a maniac man all the way through Maryland and Pennsylvania to get here, and then me seeing imaginary reporters in the hotel lobby, in my soup at a restaurant, in a bathroom at the ballpark and in my nightmares with Sauer and Thomas siccing them on me like rabid dogs, I woke on a bright sunny morning and Grace was already seated at a table in our suite at the William Penn with a full room service breakfast laid out, sipping chilled grapefruit juice.

—"I hope you like Canadian Ham and Eggs Benedict, because

I ordered you some."

I grunted, joined her at the table and nearly poured the hot cup of coffee on my head.

"You wouldn't believe the freaky nightmares I just had."

She set down her juice glass and stared at me with her usual hypnotic eyes.

—"Paulie. You simply cannot go through life being a hopeless worry-wort."

"A what?"

—"A worry-wort. It isn't good for your heart, or your mind, and certainly not for us. If your parked car suddenly rolled down a hill, smashed into a building and exploded—not that it would, naturally—what good would it do to have a nervous fit about it? Unpleasant things just happen, and then it's on to the next pleasant ones. For instance, us sitting here with this lovely breakfast, planning the next leg of our road journey up to Boston."

"Yeah, but what—"

—"Shush, Mr. Worry-wort. Read this game story here, and you'll become just as relaxed as me."

She handed me the folded over sports page of the morning *Post-Gazette.* It didn't exactly relax me, but the word amazed was kind of an understatement...

BLACKBOARDS PUT CLOCKERS IN DETENTION AGAIN

These two-game series on the schedule sort of ruin the idea of a relaxing motor trip through America. After another one-run doozy between the Clocks and Boards, we skipped out of Pittsburgh before dinner and high-tailed it east, north, and east again en route to Boston for the Bombs and Caps weekend 3-gamer, stopping at a quiet roadside motel near Schenectady which I was sure would be devoid of reporters and even newsstands. Grace was looking forward to booing the Bombs at Final Frontier Field, though I had to insist she "root against them quietly" rather than boo, for obvious reasons.

The first game in Boston was the next night, thankfully, giving us time to take a morning spin into the Berkshires of Massachusetts, and some early Autumn leaf-peeping. "Hitch is planning to shoot a comedy film up in Vermont after our next one is finished," she said, "I bet it's even prettier than here!"

"Hitchcock is making a comedy?"

—"Yes. I believe it's about a little boy who finds a mysterious dead body in the woods."

Judging from his team's latest predictably absurd win, Hitch was probably finding everything amusing...

FRIDAY THE 13TH, AND THEN SOME

—"Paulie? Why are we stopping at Our Sacred Lady of South Boston Convent? Don't we need to get to the ballgame?"

"You'll find out."

They take their Catholicity very serious in Beantown, and it just so happened to be Nun's Night at Final Frontier Field as the Bikini Bombs opened a three-game set there against the Coonskins. The perfect way to disguise Grace for the evening.

Final Frontier is a small, packed-in park built for post-Victorian midgets in 1912, and I wasn't about to take a chance on my famously missing date being recognized. She looked kinda fetching, actually, in her black and white habit duds and agreed to keep her sunglasses on even though it was a night game.

We sat in the first base grandstand, surrounded by nuns, where I stuck out like a moth-eaten Bible, but they were all Coonskin fans and Grace sure was, especially with Early Wynn facing Billy Loes and the contest quickly going the Coonskins' way again. A Ferris Fain two-run homer and solo dinger by Al Smith put them up 3-0 and had Grace out of her seat yelping politely, and then it was 5-0 Caps into the 7th when the Bombs finally got to Loes for a leadoff single and walk. A Jensen DP ball nearly ended the threat, but Schoendienst singled and Mays, a weak 0-for-3 at that point, doubled home a second run. Ernie Johnson replaced Loes and Moon botched a Berra fly for a three-base error and Phil Cavaretta tied the game with a homer!

—"Why you lousy, er…bad pitcher!" yelled Grace, staying nunnish the best she could. But the prayers in our rooting section were answered when the Bikini bullpen fell apart for the second straight day. Jim Hughes walked the bases full and Amoros put the Caps back up with a sac fly. The Bombs tied it in the 9th on a Mays double and two singles, but in the last of the 11th, Steve Ridzik, who threw a spotless 10th, coughed up a walk to Fain and Henry Aaron cold-cocked one over the Big Green Frontier Monster in left for the ballgame!

"—What a thriller!" beamed Grace as we filed out, "It makes me want to go to church!"

I voted for giant plates of fried clam bellies and schooners of beer instead, and she thankfully accepted.

THE BLEACHER CREATURE

We ended up in Final Frontier's centerfield bleachers for the second game in Boston because the walk-up crowd was huge after the Caps took the opener. Grace was back in her head scarf disguise and had adopted a pretty good Boston accent for the occasion, and the bench we sat on was a little above the jam-packed other ones. Then an overweight guy in a big Harvard sweater showed up in the third inning, sat right next to me and started eating his jumbo Frontier Frank that was smothered with onions and peppers. Grace made a face and tried not to look at him.

—"What'd I miss?" he asked. "Traffic from Worcester was

terrible."

"Not much, except the Bombs scoring four times in the 1st off Haddix. He's going for his 20th loss, y'know."

—"Yeah, I knew that."

The guy was kind of annoying, and wolfed down his dog with loud, sloppy bites. Then opened his program and began scoring the game—even though it was one third over. He peered around me between batters and looked at Grace.

—"This your first time here, miss?"

—"Nahh," she said, stretching out her Hs "Been comin' heah like forevuh."

—"Uh huh. I'm Freddie, by the way." He stuck out a meaty paw. I hesitated, then shook his hand. Grace nodded at it but wouldn't shake it.

—"Coonskins been doing some serious spoilin' lately, right?"

"Yeah," I said, trying to keep my answers short to curb the conversation.

—"They been pretty wicked," added Grace.

—"So you're a big baseball fan, miss?"

—"Yeah...Guess you figured that one out, mistuh."

He went back into his scorecard, kind of shielding it from us. I couldn't resist, and turned to him.

"Hey, how can you score a game starting in the third inning?"

—"Eh. Do it all the time. Sometimes I gotta leave early. I can figure out the details next morning from the box score."

I nodded, but was suddenly perspiring and worried. Slid closer on the bench to Grace and whispered in her ear.

"We can't stay here."

—"What? Why?"

"Because this guy ain't adding up. Nobody in this town leaves games early or arrives late. Plus anybody wearing a Harvard sweater on a Saturday in September would be either at the Harvard game or following it on the radio right now."

—"So he's strange. Just ignore him and watch the game."

"He's more than strange. He's writing in his scorecard when nothing is happening."

She took a quick glance at him while he did just that.

—"And that means what?"

I took Grace by the arm and stood her up.

—"Hey, where you guys going?" asked Freddie, spilling a few stray onions in his open program. A note paper he'd been scribbling on fluttered down between the seats and I grabbed it.

G. KELLY WITH BOSTON ACCENT! was one of the notes.

"Nice try, mac!" I said, crumpled up the note and bounced it off his head.

"Ted Mulligan, *New York World-Telegram*," he replied, "Gimme the lowdown, Paulie."

I shoved him off the bench and hustled out of the row with Grace. By the time he hoisted up his bulk and stood up we were down the ramp toward the exit gate and starting the longest part of our road trip to St. Louis a day early.

GO WEST, YOUNG MAN AND WOMAN

Our route to St. Louis took us west into New York State and clear across to Buffalo, along Lake Erie to Cleveland, down to Columbus and across to Missouri—in a little over twenty hours. Normally we would've taken our time, seen Niagara Falls and maybe stopped for an overnight in Terre Haute. But I was doing most of the driving and gas-pumping and the main thing was to get as far away from as many snooping reporters as possible. I was imagining them in rest areas, and behind billboards, and in every adjoining booth in every roadside diner we ate in. I must have drank six cups of coffee and four bottles of pop to keep me awake, though Grace did get behind the wheel after a long "wonderful sleep" and calmly take us another 400 miles.

Luckily the first Flipsides game against the Clock Rockers wasn't until Monday night, so we had extra time to get there. It was also a good thing I had a decent radio, so we could follow a few Sunday baseball broadcasts that crackled in and out and pick up details of the other games and lean back in Polly's comfy leather seats with the top down and feast on the beautiful skies and endless fields and hills.

"This sure beats being trapped in a sweaty stadium box, Paulie." said Grace somewhere in Ohio.

She got that right.

Home of 1954 Freaks League Baseball

OZZIE & HARRIET DIVISION				RICKY & LUCY DIVISION			
Blackboard 7	80	68	—	Suspense Masters	89	58	—
Clock Rockers	79	69	1	Bikini Bombs	83	63	5.5
Flipsides	76	70	3	K2 Summiteers	75	72	14
Chrome Derbies	71	78	9.5	Marilyn DiMags	67	81	22.5
Lord of Big Flies	69	78	10.5	B. Lagoons Matter	63	84	26
Red Menace	69	79	11	Coonskin Caps	63	84	26

LANA TURNER

FLAME and the FLESH

PIER ANGELI · CARLOS THOMPSON

GAMES OF SUNDAY, SEPT. 15TH					
LBF	15		BKB	3	
FLP	10		CPS	6	
CRD	4		K2S	2	
BBS	3		MOS	3	
CLK	1	0	BLM	3	
RED	5	2	MDM	4	
			★Star of the Day★		
			WARREN SPAHN		

ST. LOUIS SLIDERS AND THE UNBEATABLES

The Flophouse ballpark, home of the Flipsides, was a palace compared to our accommodations in St. Louis. The well-known Chase Hotel where Grace stayed earlier this season was booked solid for an optometrist convention, so we stuffed ourselves into a room at the 40 Winks Motor Lodge just outside the city. Grace's battalion of bags barely fit through the door, and she had a little black mystery suitcase she never let me touch which she ended up sliding under the bed.

"What's in that thing, Grace?" I finally asked, "Family jewels?"

—"I should be so lucky," she said. "No, just lady things any gentleman need not concern himself with."

I let it go and reflected back on the game we saw earlier, a thorough drubbing of the Clockers by the Flips, who somehow found their offense again versus Pascual, Kemmerer, Valentine, McCall, and Minute Hands, the goofy Clocker mascot. A five-run outburst in the 2nd was followed by a three-run explosion in the 6th off Kemmerererer, including Nellie Fox's second homer all year and Duke Snider's 33rd. Nellie and Duke knocked in seven runs between them, and the Clocks were stymied by Lou Kretlow and Jim Wilson before Kinder.

Grace snoozed in her grandstand seat for most of the game, but jumped awake when I suggested we get a few Slingers afterwards. These are local hamburgers smothered with eggs, hash browns, chili and cheese I told her I'd been dying to try.

—"Yes, you very well might die from one, Paulie. I'll be content with a Coca-Cola and Salem cigarette and watching you wolf it down before I administer last rites."

So that's what we did at the 40 Winks (minus the last rites part), me taking my time with every delicious bite until she got bored with that too and opened a fashion magazine while I watched the late baseball scores on our fuzzy room television.

FLIPPIN' BASEBALL-OLOGY

There was no need for scoreboard-watching on my part (though of course I did that too), and no fashion magazine for Grace to lose herself in at the Flophouse tonight, because the game and the crowd were flat-out riveting. Following the 10-1 bashing the Flips enjoyed in the opener, I spent the minutes before the first pitch of this one giving Grace my theory on why all three Ozzie & Harriet contenders have taken turns struggling.

"Their weird offenses. The Clockers, for instance, are far and away the best team in the league at getting people aboard. They have 762 walks, 172 more than anyone. Their 56 hit by pitches are also the most. But their .258 batting average is fifth and their 122 home runs are fifth from the bottom. So they put 'em on and leave 'em there, basically."

—"Yes, or they then ground into one of their 179 double plays, second in the league, or their pitchers allow 183 home runs, the most in the league."

"Oh. I knew that too."

—'Sure you did, Paulie. And did you know that my Masters have allowed just 120 home runs, despite pitching in an easy home run park? And have grounded into only 139 double plays, also the fewest?"

I had enough egg on my face by then, so didn't answer. Then the Clockers went up there and made me look even dumber. They walked six times off Sonny Dixon in the first four innings and took a 5-0 lead after Teddy Ballgame Williams smashed homer #31 with a man aboard. It was 6-1 two innings later, Kinder had replaced Dixon, and the stands were groaning. But the "Flipper Tank", which is what they called the right field pavilion in St. Louis, had started making noise, chanting "FLIP THE SCRIPT!" and holding up hundreds of cardboard sad faces and flipping them around to reveal happy ones every time their team came to bat.

It worked. Three singles off Sullivan in the 6th made it 6-2. A Slaughter single and Fox double in the 7th cut it to 6-4. A walk and two singles in the 8th finished off Sullivan and made it 6-5. Hoyt Wilhelm rushed in with first and third, no one out and the infield in, and reliever Don Mossi slapped a single past Hatfield for the tying run, before a sac fly by Slaughter flipped the script! The park was up for grabs, and after Mossi set down the Clocks a second straight inning in the 9th, they were percentage points in front of them again! Because I knew where I stood with her, I let Grace have the final words on this one as we got back to the 40 Winks Lodge.

—"The Clockers walked 13 times, the Flipsides just twice, but they still lost that game. Their 16 runners left on base tell me you may know what you're talking about, Paulie."

"Gee thanks. Say goodnight Grace."

VERSATLITY CAN BE A VIRTUE

I pulled off Grace's sleeping mask and shook her awake. "C'mon, we're hittin' the road early for Milwaukee."

—"Why are we doing that?" she grumbled, "I've only had 33 of my 40 winks."

"Because it's Jerry Coleman Day at Marx Field! I've been reading about it, and it looks like a gas that we won't wanna miss."

Yup, we left by 7:30 like I'd planned, meaning we'd arrive for the Chrome Derbies vs. Red Menace 2 p.m. start time easy. Of course we had to order cups of coffee and a box with a vegetable omelette inside for Grace from the first diner we saw, but the morning was beautiful and the road straight and uncrowded. I weaved Polly around everyone else to make better time, and we pulled into the packed Marx Field lot ten minutes before first pitch.

Billed as a "Red Menace tribute to the glory and versatility of the heroic but unsung working man", Jerry would play all nine positions on the field, starting across the outfield, then the infield, then at catcher and pitcher for the final two innings. Coleman had never pitched a ball in his life, and to date, hadn't had a hit in nine at bats, so the crowd would be cheering his every accomplishment, and nearly every fan had been given a little red flag with Jerry's face on it upon entry.

Turns out the game was also swell. Singles by Avila and Carrasquel and an error by Kuenn gave the Menace a 1-0 lead for Carl Erskine in the 2nd. Coleman did let an easy fly drop in front of him for a single in the 1st, but he fielded nothing in center in the second. He also whiffed and flied out his first two at bats, but a Marsh walk, stolen base, and doubles by Finigan and Carrasquel put the Menace up 3-1 on Curt Simmons in the 3rd after a wild pitch put the Chromers on the board minutes earlier. An Andy Carey solo blast with Coleman at shortstop cut it to 3-2, and the teams remained scoreless for a while, with Jerry rotating to third and second, and first and catcher without incident! he also lined a clean single to left in the 5th for his first hit all year, producing a standing ovation, and walked his next two times.

Then in the last of the 8th, Simmons imploded, allowing a walk and two singles, and Lefty Ron Mrozinksi came in to face Noren and Garagiola, but Torgeson and Wertz rapped pinch singles, and it was 6-2 Menace! Coleman, whose stomach was in knots worrying about taking the mound with a slim lead in the 9th, was breathing easier. Still, he served up a Delsing single and walked Bruton with one out, then with red flags waving everywhere and the crowd chanting "JERRY! JERRY!" including me and Grace, he miraculously retired Kuenn on a force out and got big Teddy Klu on a doinky grounder to second, and the unsung working man was sung, and carried off the field by players and fans!

STUCK AT A CROSSROAD

Somewhere down Route 41, just south of Milwaukee, we got into it. I had already planned on us heading back to St. Louis to watch the big four-game set between the Flipsides and Blackboard Seven, but Grace had a more terrifying idea.

—"Oh but Paulie, we simply must go to Chicago! My Masters will be there tomorrow to play the Bikini Bombs with a chance to put our division on ice!"

"Are you serious? You'll risk us being seen at Castle Bravo by fans and even worse, hounding reporters?"

—"I can handle those press jokers, Paulie. Can't you?"

The truth was that I didn't want to risk any of the Masters players getting an eyeful of me again, especially Hank Sauer. What if he had blabbed about my "Commie note" to someone else on the club by now?

—"I have to admit I'm over the moon by how well they've been hitting and winning this month," she continued, "and think they'd be pleased as punch to see us!"

"Yeah, unless I'm the one being punched. By a big mouth reporter, I mean."

—"You are not making an ounce of sense, Paulie. Look, we're going through Chicago in half an hour. Just leave me at a reputable hotel, go to St. Louis and pick me up in a few days!"

"I ain't doing that, Grace."

She huffed, then got a thought, picked up the newspaper on the floor in front of her and snapped it open to the daily sports page.

—"Didn't you tell me your father was a Black Lagoons fan? Well, they're finishing up a series with the Bombs in Chicago this afternoon. We can make it, and then you can call him up, say hello from the road and tell him all the details!"

Man, she sure knew how to work a wayward son…

DUCK AND COVER!!

"Come on Grace, I don't like missing the first pitch!"

—"Hold your ponies…"

She was in our Chicago hotel bathroom making herself ravishing, probably with the contents of her black mystery "ladythings" case, even though all we were doing was going to a ballpark. It was all about looking good for her slugging friends in the dugout before and likely during the game, just so she could take credit for any power they unleashed on the Bikini Bombs.

But when she finally exited the bathroom, she was reading me part of a syndicated Louella Parsons column in the morning *Tribune*, headlined, IS JOE GETTING THE ITCH?

—"Apparently Marilyn Monroe is in New York City this weekend to shoot some scenes for her new picture 'The Seven Year Itch', and her Joltin' Joe of a husband may be on hand to watch." She tossed the paper aside, went to a dresser to pick out some earrings from her collection of a dozen. "Marilyn is quite the fetching talent, but I don't know how she puts up with such a goony, possessive husband like him! I sure wouldn't." I smiled and nodded, without revealing I had already escorted the fetching celeb around New York twice and even watched her dance with my pop.

Anyway, on to jam-packed Castle Bravo we went, where I chose to stay far clear of the Masters players and watch the game from an upper deck standing room spot high over third base. Steve Gromek was going for his 20th win, the Bomb Squad was hooting and hollering out in both bleachers, and outside of the visitors' dugout, there wasn't one person in the place that didn't believe the Bikinis could take at least two of the games.

Future generations of scientists and mathematicians may still be studying what then happened in the first four innings. Sauer homered on a 35% chance. Wilson singled and Thomas homered on a 20% chance. After a Morgan single, Don Liddle bunt, Adams walk and Sauer single in the 2nd, Wilson homered on a 40% chance. In the 3rd, Cunningham singled and McDougald homered on a 45% chance. In the 4th, a Wilson single and Bell double was followed by a Cunningham homer on another 20% chance.

Meanwhile, after a Jensen solo shot to lead off the Bikini 1st, the Bombs didn't get even a little hit off Don Liddle until Vern Stephens led their 6th with a pinch single, and were outhit 15-4 for the game. That's nine in a row again for the Suspensers, 18 out of 19, 39 homers hit in September, and their lead is back up to six and a half with the magic number dropped to six.

Needless to say, Grace was out reuniting and celebrating somewhere with her Suspenser pals drinking Cosmos most of the night, which was fine with me, because there were actual pennant race games in the other division that weren't flat-out sickening I could follow from the comfort of our hotel room.

IT'S DICK COLE'S WORLD. WE'RE JUST LIVING IN IT.

Grace didn't move for the first five hours of the day after partying up a storm with her Masters buddies the night before, so I let her sleep it off while I drank some high-octane coffee and took a morning walk around the Loop as chipper as a jaybird. The second Masters game at Castle Bravo against the shell-shocked Bikini Bombs was at 1:30, and after leaving snoring Grace a note next to her pillow, I headed over to the park on the early side to watch batting practice.

Which hardly any Masters player showed up for. Not sure if it was due to arrogance, overconfidence or the exact same hangover, but their sleepy bats carried right into the ballgame. Except for Gil McDougald, of course, who popped their 40th homer of the month into the bleachers off Early Wynn to give Herm Wehmeier a 1-0 lead in the 5th, while numerous Bikini scoring chances were disintegrating. Mays singled and doubled twice and Cavaretta had a leadoff double, but neither of them could find home plate. Still, with a six-hit shutout going and the Bombs on the verge of seeing their pennant chances all but vanish, Herm issued a leadoff walk in the 9th to Boone. Skinner singled him to third and Jim McDonald rushed in to the rescue. He got pinch-hitter

Vern Stephens on a liner, but then Richard Roy Cole of Long Beach, California batted for reliever Hughes. Cole whacked McDonald's second pitch out to right, and Hank Sauer misplayed the ball! Boone scored, Skinner raced around third, but Hank's throw to the plate was late and the Bombs miraculously won it!

Grace never even showed up at the park, having immersed herself in a very long afternoon bath, and blamed herself for most of the evening.

—"They needed me there!" she cried, "I cost them a ten-game win streak!"

"Aw c'mon," I said, "Even a shiny new car can get bird poop on it."

Anyway, the Suspenser magic number stayed at six, and 20-game winner "Mexican Mike" Garcia would be facing Puerto Rican Rubén Gómez in the all-spicy finale.

SAY HEY AND IT AIN'T SO, JOE

By now you've likely heard about the Willie Show at Castle Bravo yesterday, where Mr. Say Hey personally took the Masters apart with a single, three home runs and seven RBIS as his Bikinis made it two of three in the series with a 10-2 blitzkrieg.

But what you don't know is how the day began and ended.

While Grace and I were eating breakfast down in a corner of the hotel restaurant and trying not to be noticed, a couple of local thieves with a nose for rumors broke into our room and stole three of Grace's suitcases with as many clothes as they could stuff in them and all of her jewelry! Grace was devastated, of course, and our fun charade of keeping undercover was over. I mean, you try calling the police sometime and not telling them who you are!

Anyway, she stuck around the hotel to socialize with the authorities, maybe thinking it would help get her stuff back quicker, and told me just to go the game that I needed to report on. By the time I got back to the hotel later, there were five messages left for me by someone named "Guiseppe Katz" with a New York area phone number to call. Upstairs, Grace had a compress on her head, was blaming the Masters loss on her non-presence again, and glumly announced we could "head off to our next pointless destination at any time." I offered to wait around at least for a day to see if her belongings turned up, but she wouldn't have it. First I had to find out who this Guiseppe Katz was and dialed his number from the room.

I recognized the voice almost immediately: drunk Joe DiMaggio.

—"It's over, Paul," he said.

"Oh. Hey Joe. What's over?"

—"Me and Marilyn, for starters. Yup. Came back from Boston a day early to see her shoot this scene from this dumb Seven Itch movie she's been making, and ya know what it was? Her standing on one of those street grates and having the wind shoot up outta the thing and practically blow her flimsy dress up over her head! Can you imagine that? Me having to look at all the other actors and crew members and Hollywood press creeps enjoying my wife's panties while they filmed the shot over and over. I can't tell ya how humiliating it was!"

"Right. Sounds awful. Did you tell her how it felt—

—"Of course I did! Over and over for hours! Told her I couldn't take what she does for a living anymore and she said 'Okay, then I can't take being married to you'—"

His voice cracked. I glanced at the bed, where Grace had her hot compress off and was staring at me.

"That's so unfortunate. I'm sorry…But you also said that something else is over?"

There was a long pause. He seemed to quickly get control of himself, and his voice darkened.

"Yeah, Paul. Your health."

'W-what's that?"

—"This young bird I know tweeted something to me the other day. Goes by the name of Schnozzo?"

"Schnozzo? You mean…the Schnozzo who worked Pop's newsstand?"

—"Know any other Schnozzos? Yeah. I knew his dad out in San Francisco. He ain't as dumb as he looks. And he made for a good spy who could keep a watch on you."

"Okay, but I don't see what—"

—"You escorted Marilyn around town twice on me, you punk! TWICE!!"

I yanked on the phone cord and pulled the thing into the bathroom, away from Grace.

"Listen, Joe. Nothing happened. She just needed a driver so I thought I'd help out—"

—"And ya didn't think to call me? I'm payin' you a good wage and you're showing my wife around town behind my back?? Well, you better be watchin' yours now."

CLICK. I hung up in shock. Instantly wondering if Joe had anything to do with our room being robbed.

—"Paulie?" asked Grace from the bed, "Who was that?"

"Just a guy from New York I know who's having problems. It's nothing."

I walked back in, put the phone on the table.

"Anyway, I was just thinking and you're right. Let's get out of Chicago first thing in the morning."

A GRACELESS EXIT

There was no word from the authorities about Grace's belongings when we got up. We had a full day to drive the 300 or so miles to Cincinnati, where the Clock Rockers were scheduled to play a series with the Big Flies, but after that scary call from drunk, angry Joe the night before I was pacing around the hotel room waiting for Grace like an expecting dad. On top of that, a bunch of reporters had heard about the robbery, and they had taken over the lobby, forcing us to go down a service elevator and wait in the alley behind the hotel for the garage guy to pull Polly around the corner.

—"Why are you such a nervous nellie, Paulie? You've been like this since that phone call last night."

"Just wanna hit the road, that's all."

—"Yes, but why? You said yourself we only have a four and a half hour drive, and you won't even let us get breakfast!"

I didn't answer, paced around some more. She walked straight up to my face.

—"Who was that on the phone, Paulie? And don't tell me it was a friend because it wasn't, and Giuseppe Katz has GOT to be a made-up name."

"Please let this go, Grace—"

—"No I won't, because you're being a secretive ass about it, and you know I don't like secrets—"

"It was Joe DiMaggio, okay? And I was working for him, and now he's blaming me for his marriage falling apart because he just found out I escorted his wife around town a few days."

Grace's blue eyes nearly popped out of her head. And it wasn't because of the Marilyn thing.

—"What do you mean you were working for him?"

So I told her. About the good extra money I made trying to put the whammy on the Masters for him, and the note about Grace being a Commie I dropped in Sauer's front seat, and that I felt awful doing it especially after I got chummy with her on July 4th, and that I was afraid to tell her and now I couldn't apologize enough.

She stared at me and simmered for a good ten seconds, her fancy shoes practically melting into the cracked alley asphalt. Then turned and walked toward the hotel back door.

"Grace, c'mon! I said I'm sorry!!"

—"The Masters bus leaves in ten minutes. I believe I can make it."

"What are you do—"

—"I'm flying back to New York with the team. Do let me know if my things turn up. Goodbye, Paulie."

And she disappeared through the door. The garage guy pulled into the alley with my Plymouth at that very moment. It would be a long and lonely four and a half hours to Cincinnati.

WAY MORE GERMANS THAN ITALIANS

My room at the Fleabag Lodge or whatever it was called outside Cincy was the perfect place to drown my Grace-less sorrows in beer. The curvy Ohio hills that took me there nearly lulled me to sleep, and I had to find some loud hepcat music on the car radio to keep my eyes on the road.

The first big Clockers game at Crosley Crush Field was fabulous entertainment, though, and it was actually a relief to just sit in the stands and take it all in. Naturally, being the full-time paranoid person I am, I was sure DiMaggio's toughest Italian friends were tailing me and watching my every move inside the ballpark, waiting for the right second to stomp me into the cement. When Gil Hodges belted his 42nd homer, though with Bauer aboard for a 2-0 Big Flies lead on Pascual, the stands erupted in beer showers and German songs, and I remembered how rough and Teutonic the citizens of Cincinnati tended to be.

But Teddy Ballgame Williams seized power soon after that, clubbing his 34th homer with two aboard in the 5th to put the Clocks ahead by two runs. The Big Flies soon tied it, but in the top of the 8th, bench catcher Matt Batts batted for Kemmerer with Logan aboard and crushed a two-out, two-run homer for the eventual win and game and a half lead on the Blackboards! The surrounding Germans were unhappy, but they provided a fine shield for me as I slipped down the exit ramp and down the shady block where I'd parked Polly.

WINDING UP THE CLOCK ROCKERS

It was my second day in the Crosley Crush grandstand, and despite the disappointed crowd of about 14,000—a good many of those Clock Rocker rooters who had journeyed down from Detroit—I was in heaven. The sun was on my face, I held a knockwurst and frosty cup of beer, my T-shirt sleeves and dungaree cuffs were rolled up, and I sat there in awe and watched the Clockers take apart poor Sal Maglie for four runs in the very first inning with a Ted Williams double and Clint Courtney triple being the biggest blows. Alex Kellner threw pretty well for him, until Gil Hodges' 43rd tater tightened the score and brought on Windy McCall and Wilhelm for three and a third of two-hit relief. It was Hoyt's 27th save, nudging him past Don Mossi in that department, and the magic Clocker number for the Ozzie and Harriet pennant was suddenly at five!

Later, I rang the hotel in Chicago for any news on Grace's stolen belongings, and would ya believe it? The cops actually nabbed the two local creeps who had done the deed and recovered everything! My plan was to shoot back to the Windy City after the Thursday afternoon game, grab the stuff and get it back to Grace in Brooklyn during their big final series with the Bikini Bombs. I guess I had one desperate apology left in me…

THE NITTY AND THE GRITTY

Things didn't look too Clockish in the opening inning of their season series finale with the Big Flies. Ashburn got thrown out at home trying to score on a Skowron sac fly despite a 90% safe chance, and then a Schmitz wild pitch on a 15% chance helped set up a Doby RBI single to put the home Flies up 1-0. But then the Clocker Crush Crew took over and pulled out the three-game sweep. Dingers by Hemus and Skowron in the 3rd off Russ

Meyer put them ahead, before a Logan solo shot and pinch-hit Campanella bomb with two aboard in the 7th iced it, to drop the Clocker magic second hand down to four. After a day off, they'll play two in Baltimore with the Chromers before finishing up at home with the barely-alive Flipsides.

As threatened, after the game I drove back to Chicago to pick up Grace's stolen luggage and jewelry at the police station. Luckily, the creeps who broke in were Polish boys and not Italian friends of DiMaggio, and they managed to open every locked piece of luggage and jewelry box except for the little black case that apparently had Grace's "lady things" inside, because it had this funny combination dial on it. That was weird, but I had no time for safecracking so tossed everything in Polly's trunk and hit the highway back to New York, figuring I'd pass a decent flower shop along the way...

BOMBS SQUAD SHATTERS REAR WINDOWS

Fifteen minutes into Pennsylvania I had a dark thought: What if all this "driving Grace's things to New York" business was a waste of time? What if she didn't want to hear from me ever again? What if she had already split town again to film that new movie in France with Hitch? To soothe my willies, I called Pop from a pay phone in the first roadside diner I stopped at for dinner.

—"Oh, hi Paulie. Are you and your latest famous girlfriend married yet?"

"Not really. In fact we're currently on the outs for me not being straight with her about stuff. So I guess I wanna know if she or anyone else has called the house looking for me."

—"Nope. Though I did read a strange quote of hers in the *Eagle* after they lost to the Bikinis yesterday. Hold on a sec..."

There was a pause, and I heard a newspaper page rustling.

—"This is her: 'When we were in Chicago some personal

belongings were robbed from my hotel room, and I've been too distracted to work with the boys on their hitting again. It's certainly showing in the results.'"

Well now, I thought. Getting these suitcases and jewelry back to her was suddenly more crucial than I thought it was. I wished Pop good luck in his Lagoons' final series with the Coonskins, then wolfed down my diner meat loaf, bought myself a giant coffee to go, and hit the old turnpike again.

THE CASE OF THE LITTLE CASE

When dawn broke today, I was jagged up on java and Polly was happily weaving around cars through upper New York State. If traffic stayed light I'd have no problem getting to Brooklyn for the 2 p.m. start time for the third Masters game with the Bombs.

Which was when the fog bank rolled across the farmland a half hour west of Schenectady and covered the highway in front of me. I slowed to 35 miles per hour, did my best to keep chugging around cars and dairy trucks—and then suddenly had to stomp on the brake. At least ten cars were stopped on the road in front of me! I just missed hitting them, but the Dodge station wagon behind me had crappier brakes, and their screeching sound was long and horrible. The wagon's front bumper rammed into my trunk, spun the Plymouth around and sent her into a roadside ditch.

My mouth hit my steering wheel, cracking a tooth, but I was okay. Climbed out of the car somehow and went around to see if the family in the Dodge was okay. They were, but as we stood there we could hear other cars braking behind us, joining the pileup, and I knew this would be a long delay.

The impact had sprung open my trunk and ejected Grace's suitcases through the air. Many of them had opened, and some of her clothing items were scattered in the dish. I did my best to collect them all.

Then I saw Grace's little black case. It had struck a big rock a few yards away, mangling the teeny lock and combination dial in front that the robbers couldn't figure out. I turned the thing over, worked it for a few seconds and the case popped opened in my hand.

These were not "lady things" at all. They were strange bags of herbs and roots. Half-used candles. A deck of Tarot cards. Strange glass bottles containing bird and rodent parts. And five cloth dolls with pins poking out of them and names stitched into their chests: B. Bombs, K2s, M. DiMaggios, C. Caps and B. Lagoons.

I stared at the case's contents in shock, and everything became crystal clear. I mean, you didn't have to be Holmes or even Watson to figure this out. Grace was not only a Hollywood actress and baseball hitting coach; she was a part-time witch! The team had been getting more luck in September than a lottery-winning Leprechaun. When she was hungover in Chicago before that second game with the Bombs she never got to conduct her pre-game spells and the Masters scored only one run and got beat by a Dick Cole double! Then the case was gone for the finale and they got creamed by eight runs. She was still without the case in Brooklyn and the Bombs had beaten them two more times! I couldn't return it yet due to the piled-up cars, so how would the third game go? More important, if the fog lifted and the road suddenly became clear, should I even bring this evil case back to her?

SEASON FINALE OF THE WITCH

By noon this morning I knew what I would say and do. After the road finally cleared and a tow truck guy hauled me out of that ditch, I spent the night in a fleabag motel south of Albany. With Grace's belongings now stuffed back in my dented-in trunk and the lid tied down with rope, I chugged into Brooklyn a half hour after the ballgame started. Every parking space around Rear Window Stadium was gone, so I paid a priest at a nearby church for a spot in an adjoining alley, ran to the park and snuck in through an unattended exit gate I was once hired to watch.

It was scoreless through two innings. I climbed up to the club level, knocked on Grace's private suite door like a nut until a guard opened it and offered to pound me into pudding.

—"Paulie!" I heard Grace exclaim, as she ran over to pull me into the suite. "Did you bring my suitcases? The team hasn't been able to score, and I really need—"

"Nice to see you too, Grace," I said.

She stared at me, breathless and quaking a bit in her fancy shoes. "Is something wrong? Did you bring them or didn't you?"

"Yeah. They're close by. Even got the little black one with the bubbling cauldron inside."

—"W-what? I don't know what you're talking about."

"Sure you do. The Masters got every kind of luck they could possibly get at the start of the year, and since the beginning of September, but that's over. No more voodoo spells on the rest of the division, Grace."

She didn't know how to respond. Suddenly there was a massive groan from the sold-out crowd, because Gil McDougald had just booted a Cavaretta grounder and the Bikini Bombs had scored twice in the 3rd. Grace grabbed my arm.

—"Please, Paulie. I know it's hard for you to understand, but I need my things—"

"I lied, okay? I tossed everything from that black case in a roadside garbage bin a hundred miles from here. No more magic help for your boys, lady. They gotta win this thing on their own now."

I shook off her arm, started for the door.

—"But Paulie! What will happen to me? And my job?"

"Frankly, my dear, I don't give a crap."

And walked out.

THE ROMANCE OF A ROOFTOP

It was sure nice to be home, laying back on my pillow and listening to Fats Domino while I smelled Mama's brisket coming from the kitchen. But then there was a sudden knock on my bedroom door and Pop was standing there, all bug-eyed.

"There's another crazy famous gal here to see you, Paulie. Should I send her away?"

I knew who it was without asking, and went out to meet Grace at the open apartment door. She looked very upset.

"You left the ballpark mid-game?" I asked. "Heard you were down 6-0 to the DiMaggios. You don't think it's because you didn't have your little black—"

—"No, Paulie. It has to do with Chet Nichols and Bill Tremel being crummy."

"I'm making brisket cacciatore!" shouted Mama from the kitchen, "and we have extra!"

Grace pulled me aside. "Is there somewhere more…private we can talk?"

I led her up two more flights to the apartment rooftop. It was sunny in the late afternoon, but a definite Autumn chill was in the air. She wrapped her expensive brown suede coat a bit tighter.

—"I just want to say… that the fate of the team and my job are not important to me, Paulie. How you and I get along from now on is, and I hated everything that's happened lately between us."

I hung my head. "Guess I do, too. I mean…I was the louse who put one over on you first, working for Joe and all and getting you in trouble with the feds."

—"Yes. Thank you for saying what I was about to." She looked out at the distant Manhattan skyline. "I think I just wanted to succeed for Hitch's ball team so badly that I lost my head, thinking silly magic spells would substitute for what little I really know about hitting."

"Oh c'mon. They've hit quite a bunch of homers even without the magic tricks."

—"Yes, but now I'm worried again. They were being no-hit by Howie Pollet when I left the park, Paulie."

Now MY eyes bugged out. I told her to wait, ran back downstairs and returned with a transistor radio. The second I found the game, Bill Renna broke up the no-hitter with a two-run shot into the bleachers. Grace let out a little whoop. She knew the magic number was down to one, and a Masters win or Bombs loss would win them the division flag. The K2s and Bombs game in Chicago was starting an hour after this one, so I went back down again and came up with two patio chairs, followed by two plates of food and a couple of beers. If there was one thing Grace and I could do without arguing, it was enjoy baseball drama.

What looked possibly joyous was the DiMaggios taking a 9-5 lead to the 9th, and Bob Purkey then allowing singles to the first three Masters hitters to load the bases with nobody out. The torrid Red Wilson batted for Hoak, and our ears were glued to the scratchy radio speaker. Red drilled one to Rosen at third, who stepped on the third base bag to double off one runner, then fired to second for a game-ending triple play! Grace slumped into my arms, and I had no choice but to hold her.

MDM 000 123 102 - 9 14 0
MOS 000 000 230 - 5 7 3
W-Pollet L-Nichols SV-Purkey
HRS: Mantle, Renna, Thomas, Morgan
GWRBI-Mantle

The Masters radio network then piped in the last part of the game at Castle Bravo, which was a scoreless duel between Turley and Wynn going to the 8th inning. I'm sure the Masters players were also listening in their clubhouse.

—"Please K2s!" Grace cried, "Do it for me!"

Jackie Robinson must have heard her 800 miles away. Already with a single and double, he rifled one into the stands for a 1-0 K2 lead and Grace let out the loudest whoop a society girl had ever whooped. The Bikinis were 11-4 against the Summits going into this one, but they couldn't do diddly with the K2 bullpen and after singles by Berra and Boone in the 9th, Bob Buhl of all people came out of the pen to face pinch-hitter Karl Olson and whiffed him for his only save of the year and send the MASTERS TO THE WORLD SERIES! Grace hugged and kissed me and I kissed her back, until we came to our senses. All over Brooklyn, horns honked, firecrackers went off and people yelled from their fire escapes and stoops. A few hours later, the neighborhood still noisy, stars came out, and we enjoyed a couple glasses of cheap champagne.

"I'm not sure we have enough in common for a big romance, Grace," I admitted, "other than baseball."

—"Seems that way," she cooed. "Meaning we'll just have to be baseball friends forever, won't we?" And we toasted that fine idea.

FURTHER SUSPENSE

Grace missed a chance to party with her Masters boys the day they clinched, so she made up for it by hosting a four-course, Division Pennant Breakfast for the team and all the beat writers at the Park Plaza Hotel. She invited me to come along, but I declined, still not convinced Sauer or Thomas or anyone else wanted to look at me in their moment of triumph.

I guess there was too much sausage, because Mike Garcia was wobbly again later, and Jim McDonald was even worse. After dingers by Cunningham and Thomas gave the Masters a 3-1 lead into the 9th, a Greengrass homer cut it to 3-2, and a two-out pinch double by John Wyrostek brought on McDonald. Walk.

Walk. Clutch Al Rosen single to score two and the DiMags had knocked off the Suspensers a second straight day.

SEASON FINALES

On Suspenseful Appreciation Day at Rear Window Stadium, I sat in the grandstand behind third base, enjoying my Super Master Frank and cup of Rheingold. Before the game, it took Hitch about five minutes to amble his way out to a micophone in front of the pitcher's mound, where he said "Good eevening" to the crowd even though it was afternoon, thanked the players for winning the division crown, then handed out an assortment of blue prizes to a dozen or so randomly picked fans.

The actual game was a relief to the sold-out throng that had seen their team get skunked twice in the last two days by the DiMaggios. After Crandall doubled in Furillo to snap a score-less duel between Bob Lemon and—yes—Chuck Stobbs in the top of the 7th, Dick Hall batted for Stobbs and doubled, Adams walked, and Hank Sauer put one in orbit for his 56th dinger of the year and basically the ballgame. Labine was shaky in the 8th but got the Marilyns in order in the 9th as the Masters finished with a whopping 97 wins and warmed up for the World Series on a more positive note.

DiMaggio himself was on hand, of course, and I ran into him afterwards when I went up to the club level to find Grace. Joe was sober and sane, thankfully, and threw a big arm around me before I could duck away.

—"No hard feelings about anything, right kid?"

"Uh, sure. If you say so. And I don't think anyone was beating the Masters this year."

—"Got that right. What're you gonna do with yourself now?"

"I don't know. Probably work at my pop's newsstand again for a while."

He crushed out his cigarette with a shiny shoe and quickly lit another one.

—"Well…Soon as my divorce goes through I've got this nutty idea about launching kind of an express coffee shop called Star-Joe. Whaddya think?"

"Sounds possible…" The door to Grace's suite opened. "I gotta run, DiMag. Good luck with your idea!"

Grace had a nice green dress on and had two assistants with her toting out her collection of retrieved suitcases.

"Uh-oh," I said, "Off to the airport?"

—"I'm afraid so. Hitch wants to get an early start on shooting while the weather's still nice in France. So I guess you'll have to tell me what happens in the World Series, Paulie."

"It's what I do best! But aren't you worried about not being around for—"

—"My boys know what they need to do by now." She gave me a nice cheek-peck. "Be a darling and come down to the clubhouse with me for a moment. Jimmy Stewart says he has something for me."

I decided to grin and bare it, and we took the private elevator down. One step into the dark locker room and the lights went on and the place erupted in cheers! THANKS, PAULIE read a banner strung across the ceiling. I was floored, Sauer and Thomas both walked up with big grins and pounded my back.

—"Thanks for fighting with Grace and sending her back to the team!" said Hank.

—"We was leaking oil until that final game with the Bombs," said Frank, "Soon as she appeared, we won going away and then the Bikinis flopped the next day."

I was invited out to dinner with them in the city, but said no and gave Grace a farewell hug as she got in a cab to the airport. No doubt she was a bit of a princess, but a real nice person at heart and I looked forward to staying friends with her for a long time.

I stopped to get a bag from my apartment, then caught a cab of my own to Grace's House in Oyster Bay. The place was dark and would be empty for a while. I walked up to the front porch, opened my bag and took out the five "voodoo dolls" of the Ricky & Lucy teams she had been sticking pins into for God knows how long. The pins were gone, along with everything else I had trashed out of her little black case, but I had held onto these. Propped them up side-by-side on the top step and left a note taped to the forehead of the Bikini Bombs doll:

MAY THESE BE YOUR
GOOD LUCK CHARMS FOREVER.
         —*Always, Paulie*

1954 WORLD SERIES

In which the Masters of Suspense defeated the Clock Rockers, five games to three. The scoresheets have been lost, but I *was* able to retrieve line scores from five of the contests. Obviously, the Masters took two of three in Games 5-7...

GAME ONE
(Rear Window Stadium, Brooklyn)
Final totals:
CLK 000 130 403 - 11 10 0
MOS 001 000 020 - 3 9 1
W-Schmitz L-Bush
GWRBI-Hemus

GAME TWO
(Rear Window Stadium, Brooklyn)
Final totals:
CLK 021 100 000 - 4 10 0
MOS 200 203 00x - 7 13 0
W-Garcia L-Sullivan SV-Stobbs
HRS: Skowron, Wilson
GWRBI-Wilson

GAME THREE
(Clock Rock Shop, Detroit)
Final totals:
MOS 001 230 000 - 6 8 0
CLK 100 000 110 - 3 6 1
W-Liddle L-Pascual SV-McDonald
HR: Thomas
GWRBI-Thomas

GAME FOUR
(Clock Rock Shop, Detroit)
Final totals:
MOS 002 000 200 - 4 6 1
CLK 023 000 02x - 7 11 3
W-Kemmerer L-Rush SV-Wilhelm
HR: Rush
GWRBI-Courtney

GAME EIGHT
(Clock Rock Shop, Detroit)
Final totals:
MOS 500 000 034 - 12 14 1
CLK 002 000 041 - 7 9 0
W-Rush L-Kemmerer SV-Stobbs
HRS: Williams, Westlake, Michaels
GWRBI-Thomas

****WORLD SERIES GAME 8 TELEGRAMS****

TO: P. RUBIN
FROM: C. GRANT
CARY HERE. IF YOU WOULD BE SO KIND AS TO
REFRAIN FROM EXCITING MY CO-STAR, OLD
CHUM, IT MIGHT HELP US FINISH THIS BLOODY
SCENE WE STARTED FILMING AT SIX THIS MORN-
ING. THANK YOU!

TO: C. GRANT
FROM: G. KELLY
WHY DON'T YOU COOL YOUR PENNY LOAFERS,
YOU OVERPRICED WAXWORK. HISTORY IS
HAPPENING HERE!

TO: P. RUBIN
FROM: A. HITCHCOCK

FINE REPORTING OF OUR CLUB'S VICTORIOUS MOMENT, YOUNG FELLOW. GRACE IS SPEECHLESS WITH JOY, AND I HAVE GIVEN HER THE REST OF THE DAY OFF TO CELEBRATE AND WILL NOT BE SUING HER FOR CONTRACT BREACH. I HAVE ALSO REPRIMANDED CARY SEVERELY FOR HIS ATTEMPTS TO THWART MISS KELLY'S DESERVED ENJOYMENT.

AS YOU CAN IMAGINE, CRICKET IS MORE MY CUP OF TEA, BUT IT WAS INDEED A PLEASURE TO HAVE OWNED THIS SPORTING CLUB. GRACE SENDS YOU HER BEST AND WILL BE CONTACTING YOU AGAIN ONCE OUR TWO MONTH SHOOTING SCHEDULE IS COMPLETED.

CHEERS! AND NOW I AM OFF FOR A QUIET EVENING AND SNIFTER AT A LOCAL BISTRO...

ABOUT THE AUTHOR

 **Jeff Polman** was not a baseball fan in 1954—only because he was born that year. After a Massachusetts upbringing and much journalism in Amherst, Boston, and Burlington, VT, he moved on to screenplay and novel writing in Los Angeles, where he still runs the Freaks League and relishes ethnic music and food.